Emma Brewster
Too Hot To Handle

By Mary Moriarty

Copyright © 2014, Mary Moriarty
Smashwords Edition

ALL RIGHTS RESERVED. This book contains material protected under International and Federal Copyright Laws and Treaties. Any unauthorized reprint or use of this material is prohibited. No part of this book may be reproduced or transmitted in any form or by any means, electronic or mechanical, including photocopying, emailing, blogging, recording, or by any digital information storage and retrieval system without express written permission from the author.

Dedication

I want to thank first my family. You all do so much for me, from the hugs when I need the support some days. I love you all!!!
To My Little Bro Rob, Robert Mccleland-Smith who was with me in the beginning of my journey as an author and I would share little tidbits and he would write to me from England and say "You better be writing Sis!" I still think of you daily and know you are watching from above. I love and miss you!! Xoxo
To my friends who I have known forever who are still in my life, who give me support. I love you!!
To my Boobie Sisters and Brothers!! You know who you are. I love you!!
To Jimmy Thomas who has helped me so much in this journey! Lastly to my Readers!! Thank you! I write for you.

Praise for Mary Moriarty
One Thousand Years to Forever

One Thousand Years to ForeverMoriarty did a wonderful job melding thousands of years of history with current day without missing a single beat. This novella is truly quite a gem. Five Star Rating and Crowned Heart for Excellence ~ InD'Tale Magazine~

True love...a strong emotion that CAN stand the test of time. In this wonderful read, Colum and Katherine are destined for one another. Every time Katherine "dies", she is reincarnated, and Colum, an Irish Vampire Prince will never stop loving her, despite having to wait for the next reincarnation to grow up!!! With her latest reincarnation, he WILL stop it from happening again. Colum is sexy and mysterious with cover model looks....what woman could say no to that!!! He is also protective, and tender...sigh.

The reader is taken through a myriad of emotions, from sadness, to happiness, and even suspense! I highly recommend this story to those hoping and looking for a love story that stands the test of time!!!!

Don't forget to read the next book in the series, "I've Been Waiting for You (My Beloved Vampire)"...it's even better!

Five Star Rating ~Susan Newman~

Katherine MacNamara is one tough lady with a lot of moxie, which has gotten her into one hot mess of a jam. Colum O'Heachthanna, a fierce Irish warrior prince, is there to save and protect her, as he evidently has tried, unsuccessfully, to do for centuries.

Colum is heir to the throne of his vampire world and Katherine is destined to be his queen, if Colum can save and turn her. There is a twist to the world of Colum O'Heachthanna, I don't want to give it away, but I LOVE IT! The attraction between Kat and Colum is all encompassing. Colum knows why, but Kat is not sure she is ready to move on and love again after the loss of her firefighter husband in the Twin Towers on 9/11. It was Colum who saved her life that day, and who made a promise to her husband that he would watch over and protect Kat and their children. Kat has vowed vengeance on those responsible for the attacks that day, and in a very public forum; which has attracted the attention of a group determined to silence her once and for all.

Several years after the loss of her husband Kat moves herself and her children to the home her deceased grandmother has left her in a small town away from the city, and its memories of that fateful day. During a morning jog she runs into Colum and discovers that they are now neighbors. Colum befriends her and their friendship quickly escalates. As Colum begins to reveal to Kat that this is not their first time together she, also, begins experiencing disjointed memories of their past lives and deep love for each other. As the attacks on Kat and her family begin in earnest, Colum vows that, this time, he will turn Kat before it is too late, and she will finally take her rightful place as his queen. Will he succeed?

This book is jam packed with intrigue, action, and plenty of steam. We get to meet all of Kat's family and much of Colum's, but I have a sense that there will be a lot more to learn about the O'Heachthanna family in coming books (I'm hoping). All those we meet in this first installment are strong, interesting characters that immediately draw you into their lives and make you want to know them better. The storyline is captivating and keeps you turning page after page until there are no more pages to turn. I guarantee it will leave you wanting to know more. I believe Ms. Moriarty very cleverly left us with a few strategic questions, hopefully to be answered in future installments and I, for one, cannot wait to read the continuing story of eternal love and devotion between Kat and Colum.

Five Star Rating ~Renee~
I've Been Waiting for You

This is really Odin and Sally's story but there is so much that goes along with that, from past, present and future it brings several stories into play. This large cast of characters are as always with Mary's work, very well developed. I found myself absolutely charmed by some while I felt the evil resonate with others. I felt the love of family, the unbridled passions of the love between mates and the inconsolable devastation of loss.

This is the continuation of the first story, " A Thousand years to Forever " Which like this one is so far from the norm of your typical paranormal, vampire romance, you just get caught up and carried along throughout the whole journey with more twists and shocking surprises. We meet spirits, witches, vamps who are part fae and or part fallen Angel who all have their own series of mad skills. Oh yeah, did I mention the terrorists? Yeah, we have them too! I am so looking forward to the next book, "Redemption at Midnight"... I just have to see what happens next!

Five Star Rating ~Anna Salamatin~

Redemption at Midnight

First off, I got to mention how much I love this cover. It was what stood out for me first. Its dark with gorgeous coloring with a title that was just as tempting as the cover. But it was the blurb that caught my attention and had me wanting to read this story.

Redemption at Midnight was brilliantly written with a strong storyline, compelling characters, and touching moments that left me completely breathless and amazed.

Bella is a GORGEOUS woman, a vampire who has never known love and wants to. We have Brent a man who was once an Ops until he lost both his lower legs and his hand in an IED blast. He is very upset and bitter over everything and thinks he is no good for anything anymore.

When Bella and Brent get together, they both learn that all it takes to heal is each other. The fact that Bella NEEDS Brent in her time of "needing" was a spectacular thing to read about.

I think this book was beautiful, touching, and down right perfect! I give Redemption at Midnight a FOUR AND A HALF OUT OF FIVE STARS! I HIGHLY suggest you pick up a copy today and read what everyone is talking about. I don't think you will be disappointed.

Four Star Rating ~Marie Brown (Marie's Tempting Reads)~

The Kings of Angkor: Army of a Thousand Elephants

The Kings of Angkor Army of a Thousand Elephants is a great story by a gifted writer. ~I was hooked from the first page.~

Exciting, intriguing, and fast paced. This book is filled with unexpected twists as you easily follow the characters through the adventure. The cultural ties between the past and present Cambodia cannot be severed or forgotten.

If you're looking for a book about people with great passions, a book that will take you away from the world you thought you knew and send you into a different reality that is totally absorbing and believable, then this is the book for you.

Five Star Review ~ Jae Hall

The Witchling Grows Up

The Prologue reads like a short story all n it's self and I was absolutely enthralled as I read about this large powerful family made up of a demi-god and witches with great powers, Two amazing children, a boy 12 yrs. older than his sister and the life they had for centuries until a new baby girl is born...and all hell breaks loose! ....And so it begins......

Will is left to raise his niece Rose with the help of cousins Emma & Molly and Molly's Mother, his Aunt Sadie. There is also a pack of cats and hounds (familiars) which they can communicate with. So, Will moves everyone to London Town where he just bought a home. The first of many properties purchased over the years as his fortunes grew. He never settled down, but spent these passing years bent on revenge against those responsible for the loss of his mother & sister the night Rose was born. Now Rose is grown and she too give birth to a baby girl. Her name is Dylan. And as Will chanted his blessing over the baby, stardust fell from the ceiling, a whirlwind came and in it a dragon! Though no larger than a crow he will watch over Dylan all her life to make sure the darkness never overtakes her. The dragon tells them that Dylan is the one foretold who will bring all creatures together. I just love Tan, the little dragon, he has such fierce loyalty throughout this story and I couldn't help but laugh at some of his antics...So Dylan, is not a normal witch, she is immortal. She has a special mark (like her mother did).....By the time she is 90, she still looks like 20 yrs. old! Right? How cool is that? But it's not all sunshine & roses, something very dark, very evil is brewing somewhere and it has it's sights set on Dylan and the unequaled power she will come into at her "time". Dylan's has been getting notes from a certain fellow.........And Uncle Will and her Mother is missing!

Justice is a warrior. He is also a Vampire.....One night he has a vision, a message from the Goddess. While looking at the moon he saw Dylan and he knew their destinies were entwined. Aunt Molly tells him he is the one to protect Dylan. As the story continues and they get to know each other, (much to the dragons chagrin I might add) Turns out they are mates! A vampire & a witch? This has never been before! and there is still the dark one closing in and hell bent on getting Dylan first. He casts a spell and it brings her to him... Has the Goddess forsaken them?

This is but a taste of all that happens, I don't want to give too much away! This is not your typical good vs. bad. And it sure ain't no fairy tale. This is Vampire, Royalty, Witches, Hell Hounds, Magic, Dark Evil and we can't forget the Dragon! This is a journey to a world where anything can happen and I for one just loved the trip!

I was given this book in return for a honest review.
Five Star Review ~ Anna Salamatin

I loved this story! I loved how Mary added her own unique take on both Dylan - Witch and Justice – Vampire as well as with Tan her dragon. I now want a dragon just like him! I loved the humor and the "power plays" between all of the characters – Tan and Justice or Justice & Max (this was my personal favorite)! All everyone wants to do is protect Dylan, and yet she doesn't understand why. Being a 90 something old virgin witch might have something to do with that innocence! I fell for both Dylan & Justice and hope to find more of their tale in Mary's My Beloved Vampire series. Even though this is a shorter book, I found that Mary did a wonderful job of providing enough details to love the story without being bored by too much "background/explaining" & not enough "story" or the opposite – not enough detail that you don't have a clue as to what is going on. This is the first book that I have read of Mary's but I fully intend to read ALL of her books.

Five Star Rating ~ Cherri-Anne Boitson

Boston Massachusetts 1690

Goody Brewster hurried along the cobbled path to her door. Picking up the latch, she gave her front door a mighty shove.

It was later than she had wanted to be out and what with it being a night before Sabbath she dared not be out late again, even if it was to help Goody Wilson with her new babe that she had delivered a fortnight ago.

After slamming her door to the wind that had blown up out of nowhere, she rushed down the hall to the kitchen in the back of the house. The house was cold and dark. *Where oh where could Papa be? He should have lit the candles...*

As she rushed into the kitchen she knew her dear Papa would be alone in his study, pouring over books, trying to find what he was looking for... if only he could remember what it was he was looking for.

Goody Brewster, or Eliza as her family and friends called her, stood and held her growing stomach. She patted it and smiled. It was the only thing besides the home her dear husband had left her. He had the misfortune of slipping and hitting his head, then being run over by a cart laden with goods bound for the docks. Even all the knowledge she had couldn't make him better. He had been clear headed for a few days and she had thought he would get well. He had insisted on making sure everything was in order so not to leave his beloved wife wanting. They didn't have much but what they did have, he wanted to make sure his Eliza was provided for.

Eliza rushed about the house lighting candles and then she took the bellows and got the coals going in the fire so to heat the stew she had still in the pot. She turned and checked the bread. *Good, plenty of bread till Monday, since she couldn't bake tonight or tomorrow. There was always someone going around checking the chimneys… or peeking in the windows…*

That thought brought a blush to her. When she and her beloved John had first been married they had not always kept to their bedchamber when they made love. And they didn't always close the shutters. They almost got caught and had they been caught it would…

"Daughter you are wool gathering again…"

Eliza turned to her Papa's voice. "Papa you forgot to light the candles for me and the fire was almost out."

Matthew Proctor walked up to his one and only daughter. He knew he was slowly losing ground but he also knew his beloved daughter was a witch, even if she did hide it well. She always denied when he asked but he knew…

"Daughter, I have been reading in my study and I thought you would be home earlier."

Eliza turned away from her Papa and went to stir

the stew. Since she knew she was blocking his view, she brought the loaf of bread that sat on the cold brick to the bricks nearest the fire. He needn't know she did that. She still didn't know why she hid the fact from him. Maybe because his instability could get her hanged if he talked to the wrong people.

Eliza turned and saw her father looking around him. *And he talked about wool gathering.*

"Papa, why don't you go sit by the fire and cover up with the blanket. I will bring your meal to you there." She pointed to his chair, then turned and put the water kettle on. They would have some tea, their last little bit till she could go purchase more. She grabbed the tin down from the shelf and saw there was really just enough for one. "Wait a moment Papa." She took her finger and, saying a few quiet words, was able to multiply the tea to last till Monday.

"I am bringing you your stew and bread." She ladled out some stew and then placed that on a tray. She brought the bread to the great table that her John had made with his own hands for her before their wedding. She cut a good slice and spread some butter she had made herself. She was lucky they had a cow.

The little boy whom they had adopted, who had lost his family on board one of the many ships bound for the new world from Scotland should be back soon. He minded the cow at the town common. Little Angus was a sweet boy and she snatched him up before some of the old biddies could and make him a slave.

Bringing the tray to her Papa, she then went back to the fire and waited for the water to come to boil. She would have her tea with her stew and bread. *Where was Angus? It was getting late. She would have to pay a fine if he got caught out again after sun down.*

As if by magic she heard the door from the shed open and she heard wee Angus's voice call "Eliza?"

Eliza knew something was wrong. She picked up her skirts and went to the back door. Looking down at Angus she saw he looked disheveled. "What happened, my little boy?"

Angus wiped the tears away. The Mather boys beat me up and took our cow…"

Eliza felt her anger coming to the tips of her fingers. She would have a very hard time keeping things from going awry. She bent down as much as she could with her growing belly.

"Tell me lad, what happened?"

Angus looked up at his adoptive mother. He was very thankful she had taken him in and she said he was just like her own son, that he would be treated just like her own in every way.

"They said hateful things about you and Grandpa and said we didn't deserve our own cow and that…that they were doing a service to the town of Boston by taking our cow."

Eliza knew there was more, she could feel it. "What else?"

Angus shuffled his feet, hoping if he waited long enough Eliza would not ask any more questions and he could have his supper.

"Angus?"

"They said things about you that weren't fit to be said or heard."

Eliza had a feeling she knew but wanted the facts straight. "What things?"

Angus felt smaller than his already small stature. "They said you were a witch and not a good woman. That you killed your husband and that you were a daughter of Beelzebub."

Eliza laughed. "That's not new news, Angus. They have been saying those things to all the women who work with herbs and deliver babies. Just because I am not a doctor like their esteemed father who is a son of the dear Reverend. Don't you worry. Now go get your supper. I will go take care of things."

"But what if you get caught out after dark. They will call you an immoral woman too."

Eliza bent and kissed the boy's head. "Don't you worry. Now go clean yourself up so you are clean for church tomorrow."

Angus knew not to question Eliza but he also knew the law. "But Eliza, the doctor hasn't given us leave to bathe."

Eliza was already putting on her cloak.

"Fiddlesticks. Build a bigger fire and after you eat put a big cauldron on for water to heat, because I think we should all bathe tonight and who knows, we may tomorrow too…"

Angus feared for Eliza. When she got like this she couldn't be talked out of whatever got into her head and her being with child.

As Eliza walked by the fire she pointed her finger out at it and saw the flame burst forth. "There, the fire is already going nicely, just feed it and I will be back soon with our cow and maybe more."

* * * *

Eliza had only to walk a few streets over to the Grand Mather residence. Her home had been built for Increase Mather after the fire of 1676. He had then moved to the house that now stood in front of her. Apparently there was company because she heard lots of voices and laughter. Eliza gathered her cloak about her and walked up the stairs and knocked on the door.

Eliza stood and was met by one of the servants. "Goody Brewster, you should have come around back…"

Eliza didn't give the servant a chance to say anything else. "What I am here about is of importance and I will never use the servants' door since I am not a servant."

She pushed past and went into the grand parlor to

the right of the door. She liked seeing the shocked looks on the faces of the people assembled. *Good.*

"What is the meaning of this? You come to my house after hours, Goody Brewster, and will be fined for being out of doors."

"I am afraid I have come with bad tidings and you will not have me fined because you have guests here who are not in their homes and your son's two boys, Reverend Mather, beat up my adoptive son and stole my cow. I am close to my time and to be bothered so by young ruffians." Eliza heard the boys' mother and grandmother gasp. *Good, those old biddies...*

"If what you say is true I will make sure they are punished properly, Goody Brewster, but you should have waited till tomorrow."

Eliza smiled inwardly as a servant was sent to bring the offending ruffians to the parlor. She would take care of them herself.

"Sit you down, Goody Brewster, and a hot beverage will be brought for you."

They waited. A hot beverage was brought to her. She planned as she sipped. She heard the commotion as the boys were brought and nearly dragged into the parlor.

"We didn't do it, we only brought the cow home because it ran away from Angus. We would return it tomorrow."

The Reverend Mather smiled as he turned back to Goody Brewster. *If only he could prove she was a witch like everyone said she was.* "I knew there was a mistake…"

Eliza put her beverage down on the small table to her right and stood. Her babe leaped in her womb. She rubbed her belly and then grabbed at her side. She knew her time was fast approaching. "Then tell me how my Angus got all the bruises and cuts to his face. He said they beat him with sticks, said lies to him about myself and then took the cow and said 'it was better off without belonging to a witch and the daughter of Beelzebub'."

Eliza enjoyed the shocked tones of the women's gasps. She then noticed for the first time a man who stood and came to her side as she grabbed at her side again.

"Can't you see, cousin, these rascals have been causing mischief, this poor woman is about to give birth and she had to come here to retrieve her property." He turned to the boys. "Shame on you, boys. I have judged many a trial where boys of your age from good families had nothing else better to do than to cause mischief. And it's quite plain as the wart on Auntie's nose that this woman here is no more a witch than you or I."

Reverend Mather gathered himself up. "Well what you say may be true but an unmarried woman shouldn't be out and about after dark."

Eliza could feel the pains getting stronger, but she would finish this up. "I remind you I am a widow, and with that have distinction among the people of Boston town. I have never asked for anything. I have provided for myself and my family by my skills as a midwife. I am not in debt and will not be to you, Reverend Mather. Now if you will give me my cow back I will leave your home." Eliza clutched at her belly, doubled over and she gasped.

Jonathan Smith turned to the young, comely woman again. "Let me assist you to your home and may I call a doctor or midwife for you as I can see you are near your time."

Eliza knew she would need his help. She was indeed in labor. She bit her lip and wiped the sweat from her brow. "Yes, thank you."

Jonathan turned. "Boys, bring the cow to Goody Brewster's home right away. I will think up a way for you to repay her."

Jonathan wrapped a protective arm around the woman and escorted her out of the parlor and was almost to the top step when he heard her moan. "I will carry you because I think you won't get much further. Where is your home?"

Eliza felt the baby move and felt her water break. "Oh…"

Jonathan could see her dilemma. He scooped her up and rushed out the door. "Where is your home?"

"Around the corner on Anne Street. The small home that once belonged to your cousin…" She gritted her teeth and arched her back in the arms of the stranger. She grasped at his coat and muttered a spell in hopes of slowing the labor. She looked up into the face of the man who was bringing her home, and somehow she knew he would not be going away from Boston anytime soon. She felt his broad chest and hard muscles and for one who practiced law he was built more like a farmer or stone mason than a lawyer or a magistrate. "You are too…" She gasped and clutched tighter to him as he knocked at her door. "Kind."

Jonathan smiled down at the woman in his arms and he knew he had found his future wife. He knew it because he had seen it when his mother had read it in the cards before he had left England. It was fortunate he was there when she had arrived. He would not allow his cousins to hold sway over people much longer. They had become too powerful and with that came greed and abuse. "Not at all… We have more in common than you may think." He finally pushed open the door and saw a young boy with a black eye and scratches on his face. "Boy, your mother needs a midwife, go quick and don't come back till you have her."

Jonathan looked down into the face of Eliza Brewster. "I have never delivered a baby but I may have to assist you should she not arrive in time."

Eliza turned her eyes up to this stranger's face. Somehow she felt he was not a total stranger. "You are…" she grabbed at his coat and directed him to the table that was in front of the hearth "Kind."

Jonathan smiled. "Yes, I know, it's providence that I happened to be there and maybe more." He saw an older fellow sleeping by the fire. "Is that your father?"

Eliza arched in the arms of her rescuer and started to bear down. "Yes…"

Jonathan placed Eliza down on the table. "I am sorry this isn't softer but we need to have you up where you can be safe from a draft."

Eliza didn't care at this point. "Please help me, the babe comes and will be too quick for Goody Proctor."

Jonathan took his coat off and rolled it up and placed it under Eliza's head. He then pushed his sleeves up and watched as she lifted her skirts and spread her legs. Lord have mercy, she was beautiful, even in labor. He would indeed marry her and have her for his wife and bedmate. But for now he must bring this babe into the world.

"The baby is crowning already. Instruct me in what I should do."

Eliza tried not to think about the fact that she was showing a strange man her nether regions. Only her husband had seen her like this and to spread her legs for a man other than her husband… She started to laugh as her contraction stopped for a second.

"What is so funny, Goody Brewster?"

Eliza spread her legs wider and took his hands. She could feel her babe ready to be born and this stranger would assist. "Ye are present to help me and seeing me in this way and we haven't been formally introduced." She gasped and swore an oath that would have shocked the Mather family. She didn't care. Let those men have a babe spread them wide open the likes only women could do. She felt Jonathan Smith's hands on her bottom. She grimaced but let her hand touch his as she guided him. She let her head go back with a scream as the baby's head moved past and came into the world and with one more push her babe was born. She lay back as Jonathan brought the babe up to her breast. She had moved her top aside so the babe could suckle for a bit. She watched as Jonathan let his finger touch her babe's face Yes, he would be her husband before the season was out.

Present Day Maine

Emma Brewster read the last pages of her great, great, well ten generations back grandmother. The First Brewster witch here in America. Eliza had indeed married Jonathan. They had settled down in Boston for a year or so and then the witch hysteria had grown to the point Jonathan knew he must get his wife out of Boston. So they had taken a ship bound for land being given to anyone who wanted to settle. They had settled what is now Mid-coast Maine for Massachusetts. Both practiced their magic and had ten more children.

What Emma was looking for was reference to the fire in Boston in 1691. Apparently since both Eliza and Jonathan practiced the old religion and they were fire-starters, when they got excited their magic also turned into fire. Sometimes their lovemaking was so fiery it got out of control and that was the real reason for the fire in 1691 that burned down many buildings on North Square and Anne Street.

Emma smiled. So she came about her strange powers naturally. To have two fire-starters in her family and many more since then, well it only made sense she was one. She had a tendency when she got excited or horny to set fires, so she stayed away from the opposite sex as much as possible.

Emma adjusted her corset so her ample breasts

were nestled more comfortably in their nest. Today it was a nice purple one and along with her skinny jeans, she was a picture. She had been so happy when corsets had come back in style. She wore them like a glove and she didn't feel any confinement from wearing them. Her closet was full of them.

She got up off the window seat. Looking out the window she saw the bright blue sky of the beginning of October. Living on Magnolia Street, October was the best time of year. The whole street got into decorating for Halloween and she always went over the top.

Chapter 1

Cas O' Halloran had a few spare minutes and since the Fire department was next to a great bagel shop he locked the door to the office and went out the back door to get some fresh coffee and a bagel.

It was pouring. Yesterday had been one of those beautiful autumn days and that was why he was so glad he moved to Maine. He didn't get a chance to see sky like that down in the city. There not so much, here beautiful.

He stood in line and ordered his bagel and then grabbed a cup of coffee with extra cream. He paid for everything, grabbed his bagged bagel and headed towards the door.

As he pushed open the door he banged into a red head who was hell bent on getting in out of the rain. She looked up for a fraction of a second and that's all it took. He saw her beautiful green eyes and her red hair that despite being wet, glowed. All she had on was a dark green corset to match her eyes. Under that was a white peasant blouse and popping out were the most beautiful breasts, creamy in color with rain drops on them, one making its way down her cleavage. She had on skinny jeans that fit her like a glove.

"Excuse me, but when you think you are finished ogling me would you mind terribly getting out of my way so I don't melt out here…"

Cas was dumbfounded. Did she say she would melt? He stepped to the side and let her pass. He thought he heard a cat hiss but he didn't see any around.

Emma walked past the gorgeous man who she realized was the new firefighter that the town hired. She had seen the article in the paper about needing another full-time man. He was one handsome man. She looked down at the floor and realized her familiar cat, Midnight, was beside her. But since he was also a changeling he had made himself invisible. "Midnight!" she hissed. He looked up at her with one of his bored looks and flicked his tail at her and went to the back.

"Miss?"

Emma looked up at the girl behind the counter, who was staring at her with a funny look. "Sorry…" Emma walked up and tried to still her machine gun beating heart so she could place her order. She felt her body all twitchy, and then her fingers started to feel like sparklers on the Fourth of July. She stuffed her hands in her pockets and waited for her order. Better to quiet the sparks than to let people see her hands lighting up and going off like a Roman candle.

"Miss your order comes to $9.45."

Emma sent a silent prayer to the Goddess and pulled her hands out. *Good, no sparks.*

She doled out the money and grabbed her bag,

muttering her thanks. She hoped Midnight would follow her home. She lived only a few blocks, but since it was raining she had driven her custom painted orange Fiat down so as to not get too wet. That is until that firefighter ogled her and she was getting soaked while rain poured down and he stared at her.

Running into her house, she smelled the aroma of bread dough rising. She had a few more bowls out, all with other ingredients for other things she had to bake today for different B&Bs who didn't bake for themselves.

She set her bag down and heard the cat flap open and Midnight change as he walked across the floor.

"You are really bad, you know that Midnight, don't you?"

Midnight jumped up on the counter and Emma hissed at him.

"I don't know why people hiss at cats... It doesn't really scare us. You least of all Emma."

Emma had to smile. She was really a softy when it came to Midnight. She had found him as a kitten and he had told her he was a reincarnation of her family's cat Macbeth.

"You know, don't you, that you were sending sparks?"

Emma nodded as she poured some tea and then walked to the kitchen table and sat down with her little breakfast. "I know. I had to stuff my hands in my pockets to put them out."

"It's a wonder you didn't burn those tight jeans of yours."

Emma chewed her bagel and drank her tea. "Why me? Why can't I just be an ordinary witch, or not a witch at all?"

"You were the only child of your mother. It's a great power, you just need to harness it."

Emma chewed the remainder of her bagel and remembered what she had read about Eliza Brewster. Maybe if she could find her true love. The one who wouldn't care she was a witch or a fire starter. At least then she could learn how to harness her powers. Her phone rang. Picking it up, she saw it was the new B&B that had just opened about a month ago. The Captain's House B&B was almost as old as her house. Hers was the oldest house on Magnolia Street, built back in 1790. Most of the houses on her street were built during the Victorian Era. By the 1920s, Magnolia Street was tree lined and full of families that worked in the woolen mill down in town.

"Hello this is Emma…"

"Emma, this is Sherman. I am really sorry to bother you, but would there be any way you could have some cupcakes baked for my Saturday Tea? I have a group of ghost hunters. That reservation will make my numbers top the charts."

Emma took down her pad of paper. "So how much and what flavor and what color frosting?"

She wrote and listened. "Okay, I will have them

there in your kitchen by five a.m. Yes, I will have extra little goodies on the cupcakes, too." She laughed. "No, Sherman, it's not a problem."

She hung up and looked at her list. In reality it was a piece of cake, no pun intended, but she had visions of Sherman being one of those customers who would constantly be calling for last minute treats.

She looked at Midnight and Mika Kitty, who had just walked in and batted Midnight. The two were now rolling on the old wooden floor. "Why me?" She said as she walked to her pantry.

In among the hisses and growls and yowls from the two cats, Midnight threw out a "and you think you have it bad... this demented cat is always pissed at me for being your familiar."

Chapter 2

It was after midnight, Emma's usual time for baking, when Midnight jumped up onto the chair next to her counter. He knew better than to jump on the counter when Emma was baking. He had just lost Mika 'Demented' Kitty somewhere in the basement and was sitting on *his* chair when that damn cat jumped up and sunk her claws into his neck. What was any self-respecting cat supposed to do? Say whoa baby, come get some of this cat? Or, I am here waiting for a rough time tonight? No I send her flying and silly cat that she is, then goes and jumps up on the stove, knocks over the candle and then all hell broke loose...

Emma didn't know what happened, because she had her back working at her table when she heard yowls and shrieks from the cats. Then she was trying to clean up that mess, when her pies that were in the oven boiled over too much and the juice from the pies caught fire. That started smoke pouring out of the top of the stove and then if all of that wasn't bad enough her smoke detector in the hallway went off. Lucky her, she was hard wired and that alarm was going into her security company and then straight to her county dispatch and ultimately her town's fire department.

She pulled the pies and closed the oven but that still didn't help the smoke pouring out of the top of her stove. Then her second stove started the whole process all over again. Emma looked up to the ceiling and said, "Why me?"

She raced to her cell phone and made a call into her security company.

"Yes, this is Emma Brewster of 66 Magnolia Street, Cadwell Harbor. My alarm just went off because I was baking…am baking and I don't need help." She waved her hands like she was clearing flying bugs away. It wasn't helping the smoke.

"No, I am sure I don't need any help." She listened to the person on the line. "What, they are already coming to my house?"

* * * *

Cas O'Halloran was up in the officer's seat when one of his drivers jumped into the driver's seat of their first attack engine. Four guys were in their seats out back. Cas made sure they were all buckled before issuing the "all set, let's go" order.

"This is Cadwell Harbor Engine 1 to Cadwell Dispatch, en-route to 66 Magnolia Street."

"Cadwell Dispatch, copy that. The homeowner has called back and advised that it was a cooking error."

"Copy that dispatch. We are still responding."

Cas turned to his driver operator. "When we arrive, stay put, this won't take long." He turned to the back of the engine. "Paul, take the irons, Eddie pea can. Hank and Mike have your irons ready but I think we will be fine."

They pulled up in the driveway of 66 Magnolia Street. Cas noticed the house was lit up like it was earlier rather than after midnight. "She must be a night owl," he said mostly to himself.

Jake, the driver operator started to say, "Lieutenant she is a frequent flyer," but was waved off as Cas got on the radio. " Cadwell Harbor, Engine 1, on scene. Two story wood frame construction, single family dwelling. I will be off investigating."

Cas got out, heard dispatch copy the fact he was on scene. He knew the men were behind them. As they got closer to the side door he could see smoke pouring out the door and windows. He was about to knock on the door when a woman came rushing out the door with a smoking cookie sheet in her hands. She dropped it on the ground and without a word to them went rushing back in.

"Eddie, hit that with water."

"Got it," Eddie said as he walked over and shot a stream of water at the cookie sheet.

Cas turned. "The rest of you, follow me."

Cas knocked at the screen door, could hear noises that at that moment he couldn't for the life of him identify, but it sounded like a cat fight. "Cadwell Fire Department, may I come in?"

He heard a curse and more yowls and then a cat ran full force and hit the screen full throttle. Cas could hear the guys behind him laughing. He raised his hand for quiet. They were coming to a loony tune house, he didn't need his men laughing and adding to it. He was walking in when the woman came rushing past him but without a word again shoved him to the side, her hands holding another smoking pan. He heard her say "When it rains it pours, only I wish it would."

Cas yelled for Eddie to hit that pan.

"Got it!"

Cas walked in. He could hear the cats yowling in another room and then he turned as the woman came back in. It was the first time he got a look at her. A beauty with dark red hair, average height, well built, wearing a corset. Ah, the beauty from the bagel shop.

Emma grabbed a hand towel to wipe her face and then threw it down. She was exhausted. She was going to have to whip up some magic because of this little episode. She had lost all of her baked goods but the cookies. So she was going to have to work overtime and quick to get everything done on time. She looked up and who was standing in her kitchen but that handsome fire fighter she had seen at the bagel shop. She felt her fingers start to heat up. "Shit!"

"I beg your pardon," Cas said. He saw her grab the hand towel again as she muttered something that sounded like, "you don't need to stay" and she then turned and went to the sink and thrust her hands in the water.

Cas thought she was burned so he turned to Paul. "Would you go get the first- aid kit so I can take care of her hands?"

He heard Paul say, "This should be interesting."

"Let me get a look at your hands."

Emma looked up at him from over her shoulders. "No, there is no need. I can take care of it myself."

Cas thought the way she was acting was odd, but he also heard the water bubbling, which was even more strange.

"Well if you don't mind I am going to take a look around to make sure everything is okay. I will stay on the bottom floor."

Emma didn't care where he stayed as long as it was away from her.

"Fine, great, hurry up."

Cas ignored her and walked out of the kitchen into the dining room. The table was covered with books, some that looked very old, and then there was a cookbook opened. Then he noticed her computer was opened to…

"Did you find the cause of my fire, because I didn't think it was on my computer?"

Cas turned, feeling very embarrassed for being found snooping. "I'm sorry, it's just I saw *her* at a concert once and that was the song that she re-worded for former President, Bill..."

Emma for a minute stopped being mad at the

hunky fire fighter. "I love music and saw her in concert too." She then sang the verse to one of her songs in French.

Cas stood there. He was supposed to be doing his job and instead was talking music with the beautiful red head from the bagel shop. Then she started to sing some of the song in French.

Emma got done saying those few innocent words in French and then she felt the heat spread from her fingertips through her hands and her arms and back to the fingertips and before she knew she was swearing and running for the bathroom sink and turning on the cold water. She thrust her fingers under the cold water. A stream of curses were flowing from her mouth as steam rose to the ceiling and a very perplexed firefighter stood watching her, open-mouthed.

Paul came running in holding a first aid kit and saw his lieutenant just standing there as if spellbound. He heard Emma Brewster swearing up a storm. His sister had gone to school with Emma and he knew all about Emma and how she never went out because of her fear of people finding out she was a witch, except everyone in town knew. "Hey Lieutenant, here is the first aid kit."

Cas looked over as Paul and the rest of his crew gathered near the bathroom door. One of the other guys said the house was airing out nicely and they had checked the walls with the thermal imaging camera. "Lieutenant, all clear."

Cas didn't know what to do. He had never had a call like this. It was apparent her fingers were burned but she wouldn't let him get near her. Every time he stepped closer she screamed at him to stop!

"I really think I need to look at your fingers, or at least call EMS."

Emma was trying to think clearly. She had foolishly said those words in French and then her fingers had started firing back up as she looked at the lieutenant.

"No, really I will be okay."

Cas didn't believe her. "Let me at least see them and if they look okay I will leave."

He watched her and saw her shaking. That confirmed his suspicions that she had burned her fingers. He moved closer. "Let me take a peek, please."

Emma silently sent a prayer up to the Goddess in hopes she would help her, and closing her eyes, she turned and sucked in her breath. She felt the firefighter take her hands in his and gently touch her fingers and hands. As long as she didn't look at him, any part of him, she was safe. She heard him ask for salve and then felt him spread some cream on her fingers. She took a chance when he let go of her hands and opened her eyes and saw his turn out gear. She saw her friend Kathy's brother Paul and saw him wink. She was immune to his looks. She stuck her tongue out at him. Then she saw the handsome firefighter turn back towards her. She closed her eyes again, tight.

"I'm going to wrap your fingers up. I think you better not do any more baking tonight. If they are still in pain in the morning, see your family doctor." He gently wrapped her fingers and then stood watching her. He saw her eyes closed and she was biting her bottom lip and thought she must be in pain. But the look on her face made his heart do a skip.

"Are you okay?"

Emma was having all she could do to not catch fire or set him on fire. "Yes, if you could just give me some space I will be right out."

Cas sighed a sigh of relief. "Sure thing. I will be in your kitchen. Do you have a piece of paper that I can write down information?"

Emma nodded. "Ask Paul, he will get it for you."

Cas was going to say something when he stopped, looked at Paul and saw his smirk.

Paul laughed as they walked back through the dining room. "It's not what you think Lieutenant, not that I wouldn't mind but she was never interested. She is best friends with my sister Kathy. I pretty much grew up in the house. We were neighbors until my folks moved to Florida and hers started traveling."

For some reason Cas was relived to hear what Paul said. "So is she dating?"

Paul shook his head. "No, not now. She did when

she went away to college but said it ended bad and left a bad taste in her mouth. She doesn't go out much, unless it's to knitting groups or book sales and she loves yard and estate sales. She has added more antiques since her parents left."

Cas took the paper that was handed to him and started writing down the address, "What's her name?"

"Emma Brewster, age 30, baker, beautiful, single and a recluse."

Cas turned and looked over at his firefighter. "TMI."

Paul smiled and shrugged.

Emma looked in her medicine cabinet and found her colored eye contacts. She put some eye drops on them and then put them in her eyes. "Great my eyes are purple."

Mika sat on the beam above her. "You better be careful, you will torch him if you aren't watching."

Emma looked up at her young cat. "Do you think you are telling me anything I don't already know?"

She walked out of the bathroom and all of a sudden as she walked past her computer, her stereo came on with the song, the one that had been on her computer, and it was blasting. Emma thought, *this night can't get any worse if it tried.* She flung her hands out at the stereo but instead of turning off, only went louder.

Cas turned towards the dining room and saw Emma Brewster walking towards them. Then her stereo came on. Funny thing she was in the middle of the room, not near anything. He saw her arms go out away from her body like a witch would do if she were casting a spell. But then the music turned up and she threw her hands up like she was quitting.

He yelled, "Here let me try to help." As he walked away from the kitchen and men, he noticed his men all dancing to the music. He threw them dirty looks so they stopped and walked out of the house laughing.

"What happened?" Cas yelled.

Emma knew, but acted like she didn't. "Not sure," she yelled back. She saw Midnight sitting on the mantle, washing his paws very calmly. Maybe too calmly. She gave him a dirty look and he jumped down, flicking his tail, the music turned off.

Cas looked around the dining room. This house must be over two hundred years old. "Maybe your wiring? I'm a master electrician, maybe I could look to make sure all your wiring is okay. It would be good to make sure you don't have any shorts."

Emma knew some of her wiring was old but she didn't need this handsome guy around any more than he was now. She was going to have to get rid of him. She saw Midnight out of the corner of her eye, and if a cat could look like he was grinning Midnight was grinning. Next, she saw Mika walk next to him and the two looked like they were talking. Then before she could say *let's go to the kitchen and talk*, the music came back on and if that wasn't bad enough the lights flickered and then went off. She stumbled into the firefighter and she felt his arms wrap around her. She squeaked and then swore and then said, "Sorry, I think I stepped on your foot."

Cas pulled in Emma and steadied her trembling body. She was really tiny, except her ample breasts that pushed into him. Despite his turn out coat, he felt them. His hands spanned her corset in the back that had matched her eyes, at least he had thought *it* had. Her eyes had been a pretty shade of green but then when he had seen them just before the lights flickered they looked like they were purple.

He reached up and turned on his head lamp which was attached to his helmet. Looking down he saw her eyes scrunched tight and she was biting her bottom lip again. Her lips were a pouty pink and very kissable at the moment.

Emma had to think quickly or they were both going to go up in flames because she could feel the heat coursing through her body and ending in her fingers. She raised her hands above her head and clapped her hands and the lights came back on. As she opened her eyes she saw the puzzled look on the lieutenant's face. "I have CLAP IT." She smirked as she looked towards Midnight. "Why don't we go outside and I can give you any information you need." She pushed gently away from him. The instant her body left his she felt naked and cold away from his big, warm turn out coat.

She had to get him out of the house, out into the dark so she couldn't see him clearly. She about pushed him out of the house.

Chapter 3

Kathy hadn't seen Emma in about a week. It had been a busy couple weeks with her teaching first grade. Now that it was officially October and really felt like fall, Halloween was just around the corner.

"So you met Cas 'O Halloran. Isn't he handsome?" Kathy said in between mouthfuls of Emma's chocolate chunk cookies. They were sitting in front of the fire at Emma's, both in PJs and acting like they had all their life.

"You know he is dangerously handsome. I started to catch fire two times. Your brother, wait till I see him when he isn't working."

Kathy snorted and almost choked on her cookie. She took a drink of her wine. "Paul filled me in. He said Cas talked about you when they got back to the station. First he wanted to know all about you and then he asked, 'What color are her eyes because I could have sworn they were green'?"

Emma wiped her hands and let Midnight drink from her wine. Then she patted him as he jumped down on her lap and lay out like he was worshiping the fire.

"What was I to do? I will need to start wearing sunglasses if I keep running into him. I don't know why it's only some men who really get me going. I mean I run into guys all the time and I don't start firing up like a freaking Roman candle."

Kathy looked over the cookies. She knew she shouldn't eat any more but Emma's were sinfully delicious and she couldn't help herself. She picked one and then the idea came to her. "I know why. It's like me just now picking a cookie. I know they are all delicious but I know one of them is absolutely the best. So I pick *that one*. Now you are out and about every day. You run into men all the time, you even have some that are B&B keepers. Well they just don't do it. But then you have Mr. Tall, dark and sinfully handsome who is jacked in all the right places and you are like WOW! I mean, who wouldn't turn into a fire cracker looking at him? If I had your powers I would be drawing him in with invisible string and he would never be the wiser."

Emma knew Kathy meant well but it wasn't that easy. "I could set this whole town on fire. Do you know, my great, great, well you know all the way back to 1691, she and her second husband were making love and it was so hot they set the house afire, barely escaped with what they had and their children. It caught a whole block and then some on fire. People really suspected things but even with the witch hysteria they didn't get caught because of her husband's family. That's why they moved up here. People were a little less worried about things of that nature. They were more concerned with Indian attacks. Since she was a midwife and he was a lawyer and judge they did very well for themselves. Their original house, which is up on Chestnut Street, was a gathering place for all, whether they were ministers or pagan. It was said there was a sign over the door that said *Leave your prejudices at the door, all are welcome. Amen."*

Kathy turned and lay on her stomach. "It sounds like they were ahead of their time."

Emma stretched out and laid her head back on her beanbag chair. "They just saw what happened when power and greed got the best of people. They both lived to be almost one hundred years old. They died within a week of one another. They were the first people to be buried in a family plot up on the mountain."

Kathy sighed. "I just wish you would find the one so you could settle down and not worry about your powers. It's not like they would hang you for being a witch any more."

Emma knew it would take an extra special guy to understand her powers. Till she knew for certain she had found the right one she wasn't going to let anyone know outside her small circle.

* * * *

Cas was driving his truck from his lakeside home. He had decided he would buy it. He was going to town to tell the relator when he noticed a little orange car coming down the steep hill towards him. *Now where had he seen that car before?* As he was driving up to it he saw red hair and the person in the car saw him and he then knew. It was Emma Brewster.

Emma had seen the truck but then again there were always trucks and she usually ignored them. But something told her to look close. Why she listened to that little voice was beyond her. She did and she saw and then she knew she was in trouble. She swore, rolled down her passenger window and shot a bolt out the side. She didn't think anything about it, until she was coming back from Duck Trap Village Inn and she saw the Cadwell Harbor FD blocking one side of the road and a fire policeman directing the traffic so cars didn't get too close to the fire truck that was putting out the flames along the side of the road. Right where she had sent a bolt on the side of the road had caught fire and what with the conditions being dry, well she knew things had taken off. She tried to not make eye contact with any of the guys. She saw Paul and he waved. She gave him a small smile as she scrunched down in her seat and then when she thought she was safe she saw the lieutenant. She grabbed her sunglasses and pushed them on her face and stared straight ahead as she drove past him.

"Did you see her Paul?" Cas looked up in the sky. It was cloudy. Looked like rain. They really hadn't had enough rain to combat the dryness that was left over from the summer.

Paul knew who Cas was asking about but he played dumb. "Who?"

Cas walked up and pushed his helmet back a bit. The fire was just about out. His guys were just making sure. Paul was at the pump panel so he was at a perfect angle to see traffic. "Funny, I saw her too, just about an hour or so ago, right at this spot."

"Who?"

Cas looked at Paul and thought what with the way he was looking at him and saying who twice, he sounded like an owl. "Emma what's her name."

"Oh... you mean Emma Brewster. Oh her... yeah, she has a couple inns in Ducktrap Village that she delivers to, so she was probably delivering to them."

Cas stood up at the pump panel and thought how strange it was that she one, had an orange car, the color of a pumpkin, and two that just in the spot he had seen her there was a fire. But they were both driving so she couldn't possibly have started the fire. "It's just plain strange that's all." He said mostly to himself.

* * * *

Later that week, Emma was walking down the aisle of the supermarket in town when looking up ahead she saw Cas O'Halloran. *Oh my freaking word!* She stopped pushing her cart and fished into her purse and dragged out her sunglasses. Then pretending to be as normal as can be, she continued to walk and look at her shopping list all at the same time.

Cas saw Emma up ahead but she apparently didn't see him cause she ran right into him with her cart. She didn't even look up, she said something under her breath that sounded like "people from away being in the way" and she tried to get past him.

"Emma Brewster, you just slammed your cart into mine and you can't say sorry?"

Emma knew she was being rude but her body was getting warm and she needed to get away right now. If she could get to the next aisle, which had frozen food, she could save her hands and the store. She looked up. Saw Cas's handsome face and those eyes that were a warm chocolate brown. "Oh Lieutenant O'Halloran. So sorry I rammed your cart. I need to get going, have a million and one things to do." She could feel the heat build up and she was going to be a goner if she didn't move quickly. She saw the store manager, who happened to be her cousin three times removed. "Excuse me... Hey Peter..." She dashed past Cas and ran up to her cousin. "Save me quick..." she whispered.

Peter looked at his cousin who was related far enough away that they could have dated but she had always given him the brush off. Not that he was ugly. He knew all about her powers and he understood what a man like the new lieutenant of their fire department must be thinking. But family was family.

He would help Emma. "Emma I am so glad you came in this morning, let me show you some new frozen fruit we have." He took hold of her cart and pulled her to the next aisle. She threw open a door and stuffed her hands in the freezer.

"Oh my god, am I glad to see you. I will pay for this." The bag was coming to room temperature fast.

"Too bad that wasn't fruit," Cas said as he came up behind them. "Emma let me see your hands."

Emma looked up at her cousin, who had a strange look on his face. She was trying her best to keep hold of the bag, but Cas was stronger and he was pulling on the bag, which at this point was starting to heat up and would melt. He pulled and she pulled and all of a sudden the bag pulled into two pieces and peas went all over the floor.

"See what you made me do? I know this wasn't fruit. I was grabbing these for supper." *Yuk I hate peas.*

Cas looked at the man who had a name tag that said Peter Brewster, Store Manager. Probably a cousin. "Let me introduce myself. I'm the new lieutenant of Cadwell Harbor Fire Department. I met Emma, at the bagel shop."

"Not officially," Emma said.

He nodded his head. Noticed Emma had turned away from him like she was studying something else but still holding part of the bag.

"No, not officially till the next night when we got

called to her house."

Peter took the hand offered and shook it. "I'm Emma's cousin, nice to meet you. You will be around then so you will have to get to know Emma."

"God no!" said Emma. "If you don't mind, Peter, I don't need any help with finding friends and let me remember that come Christmas when you want the cookie platter."

She waved them both off and practically ran up the aisle, looking like she was hunting for the fruit Peter had mentioned.

Emma took a quick glance at her hands and saw they had indeed melted the bag but her fingers were fine, just a little pink.

Chapter 4

Cas didn't need to guess why he was being called into his Chief's office. He knew. He had heard there were a lot of little fires cropping up. Some thought especially since it was along the roadside it was meth dealers ditching their *one pots* but they never found the evidence of one pots so DEA had cooled it in Cadwell Harbor and had gone elsewhere in Maine where they were needed. That still did not explain the increase in little fires. But Cas had his suspicions. More times than not he had been driving and it had been when he had happened to meet Emma Brewster. But there had been other times he hadn't so he couldn't for the life of him figure out what was going on. Unless people were throwing cigarette butts out their window, but they hadn't found evidence of that either.

Cas knocked on his Chief's door. He heard "come in" so he opened the door and walked in.

Chief Smith was having a talk with one of his fellow chiefs via that way of seeing their face on the computer. He could never remember what the newest online social media was. Looking over at Cas, he motioned him to sit.

"Yes, I will keep you posted. My new lieutenant is here so we are going to compare notes and maybe we can make some sense out of this, since no one else can."

He clicked his computer off and turned towards his new man. Cas O'Halloran came with many high marks and recommendations. He had gone to college for fire science. Then he had gone to the National Fire Academy and then Officer's School. He had been a firefighter for fifteen years, if he counted his Junior Fire Fighter service.

"Are you getting settled in, Cas?"

Cas nodded his head. "Yes Chief. I just signed the papers for that nice cottage on the lake."

His Chief smiled. "Great, that sounds good. Maybe you being down there will help us with our problem."

Cas was sure there was a serious problem, he just wasn't sure what it was. "I know Chief, it's the strangest thing. We have had more fires, little fires cropping up all along Turnpike Drive. I am hoping to be able to keep a watch on my off hours."

His Chief sat back and closed his eyes. "I hope we can find the key to this problem or the reason. Since your arrival we have had more little fires crop up and at first I thought it was *One Pots* being tossed. If it was in the middle of the woods I would think it was ceremonial fires by our Native American tribes close by, who celebrate and are more into keeping with the old ways. This just doesn't make any sense." He opened his eyes and sat straight up and looked over at his lieutenant. "I am not as young as I once was but I was hoping for a few more years before retirement, but this is giving me more grey hairs. Help me find the cause, Cas."

Cas was honored that his Chief was asking him. The department had an Assistant Chief but he was just a part time firefighter since he worked a forty-hour a week job. So Cas was the only other officer who worked five days a week and was on call 24/7, unless he took himself off the roll call for a couple of days. Since he had only arrived he wasn't thinking of taking any days off.

"You can count on me Chief, I will get to the bottom of this."

"I certainly hope so. There is a pattern, if we can just figure it out."

Cas saw a pattern too, but he wasn't sure if he was any closer to finding out the cause or was just imagining things. Why would Emma be starting fires when she drove down the road on Lake Shore Drive?

* * * *

Emma stood out in her front yard and along with a lot of her neighbors started to decorate their house and lawns for Halloween. Midnight was flying about the yard, disguised as a crow. He said that was the only way he got any peace because Mika kept chasing him.

Kathy and Paul said they would be coming over to help. They had done this every year since they could just about walk. Her mother had started the tradition. She had lived down in Salem, Massachusetts and had come back home to Cadwell Harbor with all kinds of ideas. That had been over thirty years ago.

The day was perfect. Emma took a deep appreciative sniff of the clean crisp air. Being on the ocean gave Cadwell Harbor its own special scent. Today it was salty ocean and dry dead leaves baking in the sun. Everyone let their leaves fall and stay so the kids could wade through them on Halloween night.

Midnight landed on the pumpkin that lay on the ground ready to be carved. Emma always bought a lot of pumpkins. Some got carved up right away, some sat and waited to be offered up for a sacrifice. Some Emma carved Halloween day so they were fresh.

Midnight loved this holiday. He had seen quite a few in his days as the Brewster's familiar, both as Macbeth and himself now. He loved the fact he could change at will. He hadn't known till one day when something upset him and he had thought how much easier it would have been to be a panther he had seen on TV. Next thing he had known he was one and Emma had locked him up so no one would see till they figured how to get him back to himself. When Emma was gone he experimented with changing at will and back. So far he had made himself into a dragon, a panther, a mouse, but that had almost ended very badly, and an owl. Now he was a crow. He sat and let the sun warm his feathers. He sat ruffling them and then tried his beak at cleaning himself.

Emma strung orange twinkle lights around her little Christmas trees out in front of her house. Then she would go do her arbor. Paul and Kathy would be arriving soon and then her cousin Peter Brewster. Halloween was not for two more weeks but the whole street had a Pre-Halloween BBQ and then they pooled their money to get a giant stash of candy for the children. It was no easy feat for their street to pull off the largest Trick or Treat on the Mid-Coast. People from miles around came to Magnolia Street, which closed down, as did the other side streets. It was a safe haven for all the littlest trick or treaters up to high school age. One area was closed off with caution tape for older kids to have shaving cream fights. It was all an attempt to keep the holiday a safe and happy one for little and big alike. Emma stood up and stretched after finishing the little trees. She stretched some more and then spied Mika stalking a bird. She turned back to get the next string of lights when she realized the bird was Midnight. "No Mika, no! Midnight!"

Midnight the crow turned and if eyes could have popped out, his eyes just about did. Just as Emma screamed "No!" for a third time Mika launched herself and caught the tail end of Midnight's tail feathers. She snarled, Midnight squawked and he flew off with a few less tail feathers.

Emma went over to Mika and picked her up. She was still holding onto the tail feathers and growling like Emma was going to try and take the feathers from her.

"Bad cat!" Mika continued to growl and Emma opened up the side door and walked into her house. She would get the feathers later. She saw Midnight coming towards her. He must have crawled through the dog door. "Well you certainly have nine lives, Midnight."

Midnight looked up at his mistress. *"Don't you dare smile. That evil cat of yours is going to be the death of me."* He swished his tail at her and Emma started to laugh.

"What's so funny? I am still trying to still my rapidly beating heart from that attack."

Emma picked up Midnight and brought him to the hallway where there was a mirror.

"See, she took your tail feathers and even turning back to yourself, it's apparent with your tail." She started to laugh again. Seeing the look on his face in the mirror she tried to stop. She turned away from the mirror and walked back into the kitchen. She saw Paul and Kathy heading towards the kitchen door so she stayed inside.

"Hey, Girlfriend!" Kathy said as she and her brother came into the kitchen.

Emma reached and gave Kathy a hug.

"What, no hug for your almost brother?" Paul said

with a grin.

Emma reached him and gave him a quick hug. Stepping back, she looked at him carefully. She could feel and hear some of his thoughts. "Okay, what are you dying to tell me Paul, my almost brother?"

Paul walked over to the coffee machine and poured a cup of coffee. He then pulled up a stool and sat at her counter. "Well there is a firefighter who really wants to meet you on a personal side. So..."

Emma caught his thought and she was shocked. "You didn't invite him, did you?"

Paul took a sip of coffee and could feel his sister staring at him, as well as Emma. Looking up he could see a range of emotions crossing Emma's face.

"Listen, you have to get out and meet someone sometime, or you can date me."

Both Kathy and Emma yelled "No!" then Kathy turned and said, "You know that would be cool to have you as a sister in-law."

Emma threw her hands up. "No on dating you Paul. You are just like a brother, it would be too weird. I have to admit, Cas is really handsome and I knew after all the little fires cropping up I had to do something so I went down to Boston for a day to see my Aunt Ernestine. I asked her for help. I mean, I am gonna burn the town down at this rate."

Paul took another sip. "Yeah, the Chief asked Cas for help with trying to figure out all about the fires."

Emma nodded. "I know, I figured. I took to taking

my parents old Ford out to do deliveries. It seems I am a magnet to him and he knows my car."

Kathy laughed as she sat down. "And who wouldn't? You have the cutest car in the whole Mid-Coast. It fits you."

Emma laughed. "It would be hard doing deliveries on my broomstick."

Paul glanced up at Emma, looking for a smile. "You're kidding, right?" He saw no smile and she just looked at him.

"Ok, you are scaring me, Emma."

Emma started to laugh and then snapped her fingers. She had a broom sail through the air and come right up to her finger tips, just within her reach, but she had stopped it with a flick of her wrist. But the broom sat there, gently bobbing in the air. Then with another flick of her wrist it went slowly up to Paul, who by then had eyes about to pop out of his head.

"Okay Emma, you made your point."

Emma moved her finger a bit and the broom stood straight up and parked itself.

"You see, I can control some things, but being an apparent fire starter I can't control that element so I asked Aunt Tiny for help. She has put a spell on me to stop me from starting fires till I can figure it out or meet the one I am to be with. Someone who will understand me."

* * * *

Cas came out of the shower at the fire station. He wasn't even going to go home to get ready. Paul had asked him if he wanted to go to a community BBQ and he said sure. He said he would call with the address in a bit.

* * * *

"So you really invited him? Oh my god Paul, how could you?"

Paul got up and went to the pantry, where he saw a barrel of ribs soaking in some kinda sauce. "Great, your ribs, I always loved your ribs."

Emma looked at Kathy for help.

Kathy laughed. "Don't look at me, I would love to see you with someone, it makes sense. He is a firefighter, he can find you hot and leave you wet." She laughed at her own joke.

"Great, my two oldest friends throwing me to the wolves," Emma mumbled while Paul called Cas.

* * * *

Cas picked up his phone on the second ring. " Hello? Sure... what 66 Magnolia Street?" He listened. "Yes, of course I know where that is... I've been there twice already. Okay... if you think she won't mind. Yup, be there in twenty." Cas hung up the phone. He saw one of his guys look at him. "I've been invited to a BBQ on Magnolia."

Eddie whistled. "Not many outsiders get that invite. It's primarily for families that live on that street. Paul and his sister still own the family house, though they rent it. You will have fun, it goes into the wee hours of the morning."

Chapter 5

Paul was heaping kindling on the bonfire to get it going. Kathy was hanging lanterns that looked like ghostly white pumpkins. A whole pumpkin patch was in an area for kids to carve a pumpkin and enter it in the street wide contest. Paul saw Cas park out in the field that was attached to Emma's property. Her family moved on this piece of land back in 1790 and they kept most of the property, twenty acres that gave a nice buffer out back of her house. On one side his family's house was right next door to the right and his aunt's house was on the other side. Most folks kept ahold of their houses on this street just because it was one of the most desirable streets in the area.

Paul dropped what he was doing and went to his Lieutenant "Hey Lieutenant glad you could come to the party."

Cas looked at the activity already going on. "Well I was told this is a very exclusive party and that I was lucky for an invite."

Paul laughed and took the case of beer and rack of root beer Cas had. "You are welcome to stay at my place."

Cas laughed. "I live just out at the lake… I don't think I will need to stay at anyone's house."

Paul stretched his arm out. "Not many get invited that don't live on this street but the few that do have their keys taken away and locked up. House or street rules. If you are judged not fit to drive, you stay on Magnolia for the night whether it's curling up with a sleeping bag in Emma's barn or staying at my apartment, which is my place over there." He pointed to the converted carriage house.

Cas smiled. "Ok, whatever you want and just don't call me Lieutenant, I'm Cas. Now where is Emma? Is she hiding or is she busy? I would like to go say hi and start over with her, because I feel like every time I see her it's because of a fire."

Paul knew Emma was watching from afar to see if her aunt's spell would hold. He turned like he was scanning the already growing crowd and saw she was indeed standing back with his sister, watching and waiting.

"She's right over there, getting the ribs on the grill."

Cas said his thanks and headed over to her and Paul's sister. He heard a bluegrass band starting up. Who knew a few weeks after getting settled in he would be invited to such an exclusive party.

* * * *

"Do you see him? He is talking with my brother."

Emma kept peeking at him and was happy to see she wasn't tingling yet. If she could get through this party without mishap she would be doing great. Her aunt was a very powerful and knowledgeable witch so Emma knew she would know what to do for her.

* * * *

Ernestine Brewster sat with her fellow witches around the parlor table and drank their tea. Ernestine had lived in this Back Bay home in Boston all her adult life. After graduating from Wellesley College she married Parker Taylor of the Boston Taylors. They had been around in Boston almost as long as her Brewster family. They had been one of the few families who had known the Brewster women were witches. They had been sympathetic because the Brewster women had healed and delivered many a Taylor family member.

When Wellesley College had opened its doors in 1875, Ernestine's great grandmother had been the first of the Brewster women to attend. Being to an exclusive woman's college had brought the Brewster family back to the city where they had started out in America.

Then in 1914 a fire had broken out in the college hall that though was never explained, Ernestine knew from her great grandmother's diary it was her and some fellow witches trying to work a spell. Being fire-starter witches, they had tried unsuccessfully to put out the fire. Apparently their powers were more powerful starting the fire but to reverse their powers at that time didn't work.

"So sisters, we have a need of my niece, Emma. She is apparently starting quite a few fires in Cadwell Harbor, Maine. We need to look into the ball and see what is in her future so we can best keep her from torching the whole town."

"It reminds me when our great grandmothers were at college and they set the whole college hall up in flames."

Ernestine nodded her head. "Yes, Bess, it would appear like our grandmother's, Emma is having a hard time controlling her powers. She needs to know how to harness her powers for good."

Bess took a sip of her tea and then a little nibble of her scone. "She gets excited when she sees a boy, doesn't she?"

Ernestine cleared her throat. "I think she is past the boy stage. We must remember she is a woman and it's apparent she needs someone who will understand her. Even though she is from the area and has roots there, it doesn't mean people overlook strange happenings."

Ernestine uncovered the ball. She stood and waved her hand over the ball. "Bess, go dim the lights please."

Bess dimmed the lights and walked back and took her seat.

"Now join hands and let's see what we can find out," Ernestine said.

They all took a deep breath and waited until they saw Emma peeking out from behind her friend and then stepping back to hide. A handsome man approached Emma. Bess sucked in her breath audibly.

"Shhh!" said Ernestine.

They all watched with growing anticipation of what was to happen next.

* * * *

Emma ducked in behind Kathy and heard Kathy hiss. "Don't be a scardy cat, Emma."

Emma tried to pretend she was doing something but there really wasn't anything to do.

"Emma Brewster…" Cas saw her doing something behind her friend. He wondered if she heard him because she didn't move except to fiddle with whatever was behind Paul's sister.

"Emma Brewster?"

Emma knew she couldn't hide any longer. So far when looking at him from afar she hadn't felt anything, so she was hoping her aunt's spell held. She could almost hear her Aunt say, "I have you covered Emma, talk to him."

So she stood up straight and almost fell over because Kathy had moved at that split second.

Cas saw Emma stand up and he thought she was getting a head rush because when she went to stand she looked wobbly and then she started to fall. He moved forward and caught her. He didn't mean to hold her quite so tightly, but he did. He heard a whooshing sound like her breath was knocked out of her and when she looked up her eyes were big and very green. They matched the corset that she wore. He tried not to peek at her cleavage but it was there, just past her face and what a cleavage to see, like soft pink rose petals. He remembered in the nick of time to say something educated enough to maybe get him out of trouble for staring at her boobs again.

"Are you okay?"

Emma tried to collect herself but to be held by the handsome firefighter was a bit disconcerting. She was trying to fight the feelings she felt and the emotions from being held by someone as handsome as him. Thankfully no sparks, because she sure as heck had a lot of sparks going on down in her jeans and her who-hah. She was humming and vibrating and she was afraid that was a prelude to sparks so she pushed herself away quickly. "I'm fine, thanks."

Emma stood straight and tryied to collect her thoughts as she mentally shook herself. "Why don't you guys help get the fire wood close to the bonfire site? I think the band should be starting soon and they are going to set up in the entrance of the barn."

"Is the band bluegrass, I heard a banjo playing." Cas asked to no one in particular.

Paul told Cas to follow him as they walked to the bonfire area.

Emma saw Kathy smiling like a cat that swallowed a canary. "What's so funny? Because I can see you are dying to tell me something."

Kathy laughed as she picked up the BBQ utensils. "It's just obvious you are really attracted to him *and* you didn't catch on fire or set him afire…"

Emma tried to ignore the feelings that still remained after Cas had caught her. "I think you moved on purpose, just so he could touch me."

Kathy made a face and walked over to the patio. "I'm gonna start the grill."

Emma collected her thoughts, saw the cats running for another part of the house. Walking to the patio she saw neighbors arriving, setting up their chairs and blankets for picnic style eating. Kids ran off to the field in the back to play softball. A Frisbee went sailing by her head. She looked over at the Frisbee thrower. The young boy had a shocked look that his Frisbee came that close. "Sorry Emma, didn't mean to almost take off your head."

Emma walked up to the boy who was about ten years old. "Just take that to the field so you don't clip anyone."

The boy stood where he was, looking up to her. "When will we carve pumpkins?"

She ruffled his hair. "Soon as more people arrive. I will get us started."

The boy smiled and as he ran off he yelled over his shoulder "Cool, thanks!"

"I'll ring the bell when it's time." Emma said.

* * * *

Cas helped Paul with the firewood. He could see the blue grass band setting up, just inside the barn. He liked blue grass music and it fit this time of year.

"Emma seems more relaxed tonight."

Paul looked over at his Lieutenant "She is usually pretty relaxed this time of year. It's her favorite time of year."

Cas had to admit, it was his too. For whatever reason he had always loved Halloween and this time of year with the crisp air and the cooler nights it made him think of all the stories his family used to tell around camp fires about ghosts and witches. It added a lot more fun to the whole season.

"Paul, have you ever thought about ghosts, witches and things that go bump in the night?"

Paul let go of the last armload of firewood. Glancing over at Cas, he wondered what he might know, surmise or believe. He knew there were ghosts. Emma's departed family all visited the family home on one occasion or another. As far as witches, he had been watching Emma since she could barely walk. Their mother's had always gotten together for the kids to play and she started at an early age making things happen without her even trying.

"Yea, I do. Who doesn't here in Maine? Our towns

on the coast have their fair share of ghost stories. Witches, well let's just say I am open to anything…" *that was an understatement.*

* * * *

Cas sat with Paul while they watched the girls help the children with carving pumpkins. People milled around, some balancing plates, heaped with food, others holding red disposable cups filled with their favorite beverage.

Both Cas and Paul sat nursing long necks.

"So how long have you known Emma?"

Paul took the last swig and put the bottle down. He threw another log on the fire that he and Cas were responsible for. "All my life. I was three when she and my sister were born. Our parents, living right next door to one another were good friends so we were always over here and vice versa. I was going to first grade and my sister and Emma were three. As we got older we all kinda hung out together. First it was 'watch your little sister'… then it was 'you want to go to the movies Kathy'? Which I knew would mean Emma would come along because those two have been best friends since they were babies playing in the same play pen."

Cas sat mulling this over. He had grown up in the city, an only child and his family was spread out all over the country now. He had a few cousins that he had seen on a regular basis but never anyone close. He would have loved to have had a little sister or brother. His parents… well he didn't want to think about them right now.

"So why didn't you ask her out?"

Paul glanced over at his Lieutenant "I wasn't her type… then again, no one is her type. She stays away from guys for the most part. She went away to Wellesley College, down in Boston. All the women of her family have gone there. Apparently she dated a couple guys from Harvard… that was another thing, all the women found men at Harvard but not Emma."

Cas thought about Emma as he watched her help the children. She was seated cross legged, laughing and smiling with the children. She had pumpkin on her hands and one child had slung some at her, which had made her pick up a scoop and throw it back.

Cas watched her and listened to the blue grass band warm up doing a song that he used to hear all the time. The song was "the Devil went down to…"

Cas's pager went off as did Paul's. They both jumped up and then both sat down. They had taken themselves off the roll-call, knowing they would be probably drinking. Sitting back down they listened to dispatch giving the dispatch for a large out of control grass fire at… 66 Magnolia Street.

Cas looked at Paul. "What the hell? That's this address."

Paul laughed and got up. "Come on, let's go make

a cordial visit to Miss Crabtree across the street. Chief will know who made the call. She has been a thorn in this whole Pre-Halloween festivities for years... and then some. She hates to see the families get together."

Cas followed Paul to the big old New Englander across the street from Emma's house. They walked up and Paul motioned for Cas to knock on the door.

Cas knocked on the big door with the etched glass set in the front door. Almost immediately the door opened. A very old lady with a sharp looking eyes and a nose that looked like a beak faced them. Her hair was pulled back in a sever bun. "Can I help you? Because I am waiting for the police and Fire Department."

Cas pulled himself up to his full height. "Good Evening Ma'am, I am Lieutenant Cas O'Halloran from the Cadwell Harbor FD. I wanted to come over and let you know myself and FF Paul..."

"I want to see the Fire Chief and the police, not some lieutenant who is drinking and involving himself with that witch over there... you know they are involved in the dark arts over there don't you. Every year the same thing happens. She has this supposed block party and it's really to hide what she is actually doing."

Cas turned towards Paul. Paul stepped closer. "Miss Crabtree, you remember who I am, I'm Paul."

Miss Crabtree knew her eyes were failing but not so bad that she couldn't see who stood in front of her.

"Yes Paul, I see you and I know you go to this party every year, only because you have been hexed by that Brewster family. Since you were born your parents have been friends with Emma Brewster's family. My family came here soon after the Brewster women. There is something not right with that family. They are witches you know." She looked back at Cas who shrugged his shoulders.

"I'm sorry Ma'am but I am new to this town and I…"

She wagged her finger at him. "They have been involved in the dark arts ever since Boston… I know, my family came from Boston and we were sent up here to get rid of those witches but they just keep living…One of these days I will get that Emma Brewster and she will be the last of the Brewster Witches."

All of them turned to the sound of the fire engine that pulled up in the street. Cas was happy to see his Chief. "If you will excuse me, Miss Crabtree, I will go talk with my Chief."

As he and Paul walked off down the walkway Cas turned slightly. "Bats in the belfry?"

Paul chuckled. "Yes and no…"

Cas looked at Paul for a second and then heard his Chief say, "Cas, need to talk with you."

"Hold that thought." Cas said to Paul.

Paul thought as they walked towards the engine he needed to think of something to get Cas's attention off Miss Crabtree's accusations of Emma.

Cas saw the Utility 1 pull up and wondered why that was being brought here. "Hey, Chief."

Chief Smith had been at it for more than forty years and he wanted to retire. Days when he had to deal with the likes of Miss Crabtree he wanted to take to the hills. He saw Paul and Cas had already been to talk to his number one complainant, he knew the history. Miss Crabtree was as old as Emma's grandmother, who now lived in the lap of luxury down at a condo in Naples Florida. She had been crying witch for years. Apparently all the Crabtrees had. He had checked the records. As long as there had been Brewster women in Cadwell Harbor, there had been a Crabtree accusing them of being a witch. He didn't know what Cas knew, but he didn't want to scare him off. He was the best that he had for a future Chief.

"Glad you and Paul came over to Miss Crabtree's home. I'm going to leave the Utility here to calm her nerves."

Cas looked back at the house of Miss Crabtree cause he could still hear her saying, "She is a witch and no one listens. Someone has to do something or she has to pay."

Cas moved in closer to his Chief. "I take it there is bad blood."

Chief thought, *if only you knew...* "Yeah, you could say that. It's been an ongoing problem for me every year and that of my predecessors."

Cas smiled and patted his chief on the back. "I have it covered. I'm staying at Paul's tonight so we both are on call as far as this street is concerned."

Chief Smith sighed a great sigh of relief. He knew he had a good man in Cas. If he could just survive Emma Brewster and Miss Crabtree without taking to the hills. "Good, that makes me feel one hundred percent better. I will see you Monday."

* * * *

Aunt Ernestine watched, as did the others of her coven. They could see quite clearly from her crystal. Violet Crabtree was doing what she normally did, complain and throw accusations around. Her ancestors had been some of the chief accusers in the Salem Witch Trials and then they had moved up to Cadwell Harbor because their witch hunting abilities had honed in on Eliza Brewster's scent. Nowadays people didn't worry about witches. Either you believed or you figured people could believe what they wanted or belong to whatever religious group they wanted, whether it be Pagan or Christian.

"I'd like to put a silence spell on that old hag. Her family has been around long enough and bothering us in our coven for too long."

"How old is she anyway?" One older woman who was plump with snow white hair that fell below her waist asked. All the women of various ages had their hair down.

Aunt Ernestine smiled a knowing smile. "Don't worry, she is going to an assisted care facility soon. I heard from my friend who is the director that she is getting too old to live by herself and needs to be where she can be safe and sound. They are just finishing the paperwork up. Then she will be away from the general population and we won't have to watch her."

Another woman sat back from the crystal and took a sip of her tea. She then took out her own *Book of Shadows* and went through the pages. "There has to be something here to hurry that director up. I don't feel like Emma is safe with that Crabtree on the loose."

Ernestine wagged her finger at her friend. "No more spell casting on Violet Crabtree. She is being taken care of by Nancy. She won't let anything happen to Emma."

Ernestine looked in the crystal and could see things working just as she had wanted. The night was progressing just as she planned. Pretty soon she wouldn't have to use any magic with her niece and young man. She hummed a little tune to go with the music that was being played. Picking up the bowl of hair clippings and cloth, she stirred her finger in it and saw Emma fall into that handsome firefighter. The other women who watched the crystal laughed and clapped their hands with glee.

* * * *

Emma had been dancing along with others in the contra dance. All of a sudden she slipped and fell into Cas. He caught her up and pulled her in. Like magic the music changed. Emma looked up into the sky and stuck her tongue out and could almost hear her aunt and her coven laughing.

Cas pulled Emma in closer and adjusted her to the slower dance. Emma felt her cheeks go scarlet. Boy oh boy, this guy was holding her and instead of her starting a fire, the most she felt was her panties getting wet and it wasn't because she had peed her pants, but she was getting really horny. This wasn't a real romantic song but it was the first time she was so close to a man for any length of time. Looking up she saw his eyes, dark brown, like sinfully delicious chocolate that she wanted to just pour into her mouth and over her body. She could just picture him pouring chocolate on her naked body, his eight o'clock shadow forming on his face. She wanted to reach up and without even thinking, she did. She knew that was courtesy of her aunt and her witches down in Boston. *"I sure as hell hope you stop watching if something happens Aunty..."*

She heard a laugh and then, "Of course dear whatever you want..."

Touching his face was way too quick for her. She had hardly been in the company of men for the simple reason she knew what would happen if they touched. Now she was in the arms of the new firefighter and his arms around her felt wonderfully hard.

"You're a good dancer, Emma."

Emma smiled shyly at Cas. "I like to dance, love music as you know."

The music ended and the band said they were going to take a ten minute break.

"That was a quick set," Cas said.

Emma smiled and pulled him with her to the keg. "They play till the early morning hours. The whole neighborhood is here and no one complains…"

"Except your one neighbor, Miss Crabtree."

Emma nodded. She poured Cas some beer and then some for herself. They stood for a moment staring at the fire.

Her cousin Peter along with his date came up and got refills of their drinks, then Paul and his date, from one of the neighboring towns' police department. Kathy was standing next to a friend. Emma felt a little self-conscious standing next to Cas.

Cas could see things had turned a bit awkward so he tried to think of something to break the ice. Turning to his partner, he saw her swirling her beer. "So how long have you been baking for the inns?"

Emma was glad for a chance to talk about something. "About eight years. Right after college.

My parents wanted to go traveling and the house was here all by itself and lonely…"

Cas laughed. "It's the first time I have heard of a house lonely."

Emma glanced up at the tall, well-built firefighter. "Houses that have been around as long as mine have their own personality. They do get lonely. I was tired of the city, though I love Boston. That's where my family first landed back in the 1600s."

Cas smiled and took the last sip of his beer. Taking Emma's cup, he put them down on the picnic table nearest them as the music started back up.

"Well I'm glad you came back up here. I think Cadwell Harbor would be pretty boring if you weren't here."

They danced, drank and ate till around 2 a.m. Their group that consisted of eight had danced together pretty much the whole night. Things started to get quiet, so people started to leave with sleeping children. Emma turned to her group. "How about I cook us up something?"

Kathy came and wrapped her arms around her best friend. "Oh good! Emma makes the BEST everything!" Then she giggled because she thought how that must sound. Kathy saw Cas the firefighter smiling at Emma. Then she saw Emma look down at the ground.

Emma walked into her house and told everyone to get seated and she would whip something up. "Kathy

I need your help."

Kathy gave her date a quick kiss on the cheek and walked off ahead of Emma to the kitchen.

Cas said he would be right back and needed to use the bathroom.

Paul had his arm around a girl he had been waiting on for a year and said, "It's just down the hall… remember from our calls?"

Cas nodded "Yea, I remember." He walked in, flicked on the switch and closed the door. He was happily taking a leak when he heard a thump. A black and orange cat, landed on the shelf right above the toilet. "What the hell?" he said after the cat startled him He saw the cat studying him with great big green eyes and swishing her tail. Then another cat jumped down. Cas finished up rather quickly. He figured he better get out quick because the bigger of the two cats which was solid black, with even bigger eyes, started meowing and that made the other one start up. They were both making such a ruckus, Cas figured he had bothered them for whatever reason.

Midnight had seen the male come in and relive himself when Mica had jumped down. They had known this would be the best place to get a chance to talk with him.

" What are your intentions with our Emma?" asked Midnight.

"Do you think she is easy?" asked Mika. She swished her tail and gave the human named Cas the

eye. He was a hot one... *If only I was a changeling like Midnight.*

"She is our human and our witch so you better take care and treat her with respect that she deserves," Midnight said again.

Cas backed his way out of the bathroom and quickly walked through the dining room into the kitchen where Emma stood under the lights that hung over the work island. The light fell on her hair just right and made her glow. When she looked up at him she gave him a small smile.

All of a sudden Cas felt something winding around his ankle. He looked down and saw the back and orange cat. She meowed at him and it almost sounded like "Hello."

He bent to pat the cat and she reached up, arching her back to be patted. "Nice kitty."

He felt a hand on his shoulder and looking up, saw it was Emma.

"Be careful. She isn't always so sweet. I don't know what has gotten into her lately, she has been quite a bitch, excuse my French."

Cas straightened up. "Your French is excused. I've had cats all my life till about six months ago, my old tom, named Jerry passed on to kitty heaven."

Emma felt sad for him. Even though her cats could be a handful, she loved them and would do anything for them. "I don't know what I would do without mine. They are such good company."

She turned back to the rest of her guests. "I have muffins in the oven that should be about ready and I have Paul cutting up the vegetables for the omelets. I hope you like omelets, Cas."

As Emma turned, Cas saw clearly how beautiful she was and he felt himself getting a hard on. *Great, I don't need to look like a caveman here.*

He willed his cock to shrink. But seeing Emma in front of him with flour on her nose and her pert breasts pushed up out of her corset made him want to bury his head in them and just stay that way for a while. *God those thoughts are not going to help my hard on at all.*

"Um, yes, love anything I am sure that you whip up." *Boy that sounded lame.*

* * * *

Cas stood next to Emma on her door stoop and knew Paul had left to walk over to his carriage house home next door. "I've had a really nice time. Thanks for allowing me to come to this exclusive party."

Emma laughed and looked up at Cas. She was about 5"5' so he was a good seven inches taller than her. She smiled up at him. *God am I glad that spell worked...* "It was nice to have you here for something other than work."

Cas nodded. He felt like he was a young teen on his first date. "May I call you sometime, that is for a real date?"

Emma looked up and saw Cas take a step closer. Looking up into his dark chocolate brown eyes, seeing his dark hair fall over into his eyes, made her want to push it back. Hell, she wanted to run her fingers through his hair. Then she had visions, some that she had never had before. She looked down to the bottom step and felt his finger go under her chin.

"Hey, earth to Emma."

"Yes..." she said in a breathless whisper. Afraid she would burst in to flame because her who-hah was burning so bad she was sure she would catch on fire and that would catch them both on fire.

Cas was going to say something but nothing came. So when in doubt, kiss the girl. So he bent and caught up her lips. Felt her hand on his chest, heard her sigh and then felt her stand on tip-toe. He pulled her in and crushed her to his chest and then he felt it. A current run through his body to hers. It must have gone through to her body because she squeaked and jumped in his arms. He gently pushed his tongue into her mouth and felt hers touch his. It was like an erotic dance.

"I want a date soon." He said against her neck as he let his lips seek her neck. Felt her arch into him and more currents, like electrical bolts going through his body to hers. He would have sworn he felt sparks shooting from his fingers. He had never felt so alive and so much electricity coming from his body with just a kiss. He felt like if he thought she would, he would pick her up right now bring her into the house and fuck her till they were both physically spent, then fall asleep next to her. Like he had found the one, but he hardly knew her except he felt like he knew her.

Emma felt electricity work through their bodies. She thought she was going to have an orgasm right there in his arms and he hadn't done anything to her yet. She wanted to pull him in and attack him, only she didn't want to seem fast. Her thoughts were going really fast though. As he let his lips find hers again she pulled away. "How about tomorrow night?"

Cas smiled as he kissed the top of her head. "I think that would be great. Any place nearby that has dancing?"

Emma nodded. "Yes, the Train Station."

Cas hugged Emma. "Okay then how about I pick you up at seven, we go out to dinner, then go out dancing?"

Emma smiled. "That sounds fine." She stood on tip-toe and kissed him lightly. She didn't feel any electricity this time but knew something was brewing. "I will see you tomorrow." She smiled at him started to go inside but felt him pull her to his body again.

"I have to see if I feel it again or if it's my imagination." He said in a low whisper.

In one fluid movement she was in his arms again and he was kissing her hard, like it was her who had instigated it rather than him. Emma had his face in her hands, kissing him hard and then he felt it. The electrical bolt hit him and he felt it all the way down to his cock, felt it get harder, if that was possible. Heard a little giggle from her. She let one hand go down to the bulge that was between them and squeeze him gently. His body reacted to that and made it worse. As he kissed her, she said against his lips, "down boy…" Then laughing, she kissed him one more time and then pulled away. "I will see you tomorrow at seven." She walked into her house and closed the door.

He stood there for a few moments and then after adjusting his boner he turned and walked down the walkway towards Paul's place.

Chapter 6

Cas woke up on the couch of Paul's carriage house apartment. He hadn't known but Paul had brought home a guest. She came out with what appeared to be one of Paul's shirts on.

"Morning, I'm Nancy, friends with Emma." She walked over to the coffee maker and poured a cup of coffee. She then walked back to the bedroom.

Cas sat up and pulled on his jeans. Then getting up went to get a cup of coffee. *Paul must have had the coffeemaker all progromed to make coffee first thing this morning. Good thinking.*

Walking over to the sliding glass door, he opened it and walked out onto the back balcony. He could look out over the back pasture that Paul's family shared with Emma. It was a quiet, peaceful morning. The birds were chirping and he watched a chipmunk going back and forth from Emma's feeders that she had out there hanging for the birds. Then he saw her two cats sit and watch the chipmunk. They looked up and saw him and then both turned and went back towards the house and the cat door. *Funny they weren't out hunting that chipmunk... unless they already got one.*

Midnight ran up the stairs to Emma's bedroom. She was still sound asleep. The one day she could sleep in and she always did. He was hungry and needed to eat. He jumped up on her face and sat there. She would wake up awfully quickly because he was blocking airflow. If a cat could grin, he was doing it.

Emma was dreaming that she was trying to find a way out of the maze, that a fire was following her and she could feel the heat and flames nipping at her heels. Then came the sensation that she couldn't breathe. She tried to push herself out of the dream because she knew *it was a dream*. As she came awake she realized a fur ball was actually sitting on her face and then she felt its claws because until she moved her eye cover she didn't know if it was Midnight or Mika. She pushed the offending cat off her face and gasped for breath and then spit out hair at the same time. Sitting up, she viewed an offended Midnight glaring at her.

"Don't you dare glare at me, you wicked cat! That's where they get the wives' tale that cats smother babies. You were trying to kill me."

Midnight sat licking his fur and gave Emma 'the look'. *"I was not trying to smother you, only trying to wake you. Since you were asleep I noticed two very important things...but I guess you don't want to know."*

Midnight gave her his best smirk and jumped down onto the floor.

Emma was sitting, straight up. "What did you notice, Midnight? You can't just leave me like this."

Midnight stopped midstride. *"Well I noticed a*

certain male looking this way this morning from Paul's balcony. He may still be there. Could be kinda like Romeo and Juliet. And I noticed much earlier a certain old hag prowling around here. I scared the living daylights out of her and I thought for a moment she dropped dead. Third I am starved!"

Midnight sat still, looking up at his Mistress Witch. She didn't sit for long.

Emma was up off the bed and running to her dormer window that looked out towards Paul's balcony and sure enough Cas was sitting looking over her way having coffee.

She ran back and put on a pair of sweats, grabbed a sweater and ran. As she ran down the stairs she yelled back. "What happened to Miss Crabtree?"

Midnight ran after Emma. *"She fell face first on her head, That's why I thought she was dead. But it was because she lost her glasses. I have them here in my bed."*

Emma stopped and looked at her familiar. "You go return them right now. I will not have her glasses here."

Midnight sat glaring at Emma. *"What if I say no?"*

Emma slipped on her other sneaker. *"What if I decided to have Mika as my familiar?"* She let that hang in the air as she walked out into the crisp morning.

Mika jumped down off the counter. She looked at her Midnight with some pity but not enough. She would give anything to be Emma's familiar... well almost. She saw the look that passed on his face. No, she would rather just have Midnight than take his place. *"Don't worry she won't do that, Midnight, and I wouldn't accept the title."*

Midnight looked over at the younger cat. *"Thank you. I appreciate it. We have to keep a vigil on that old Miss Crabtree. She is up to no good and I don't like it."*

* * * *

Emma walked outside and saw Cas noticed her. She heard him call her name.

"Hey Emma, want a cup of coffee?"

Emma smiled. "Yes, sounds great, I will be right up."

She walked down her drive to the next driveway and up to Paul's carriage house. They used to play in here as kids. It had housed all the original carriages and harnesses from a bygone era.

Knocking on the door and then letting herself in, she was pleased to see Cas greeting her with a cup of coffee and a smile.

"Wow, service with a smile."

Cas liked her early morning, rumpled look. She looked cozy in her sweater and sweats. "Want to go sit on the deck? It's really nice out there, not too cool."

Emma smiled and nodded her head. She felt a bit shy after last night. This was actually good. She could also see if her aunt's spell was still holding. She heard her Aunt in her thoughts. She must be at her crystal early this morning. *"Of course Dearie, you know I can take care of things. Also, beware of Violet from across the street, Midnight let me know he spotted her skulking around your house."*

Emma smiled as she followed Cas out onto the deck. *"Thanks Aunty and I will."*

* * * *

They sat in silence, both with their feet up and sipping at their coffee. Emma looked over at Cas as he smiled at her.

"So…" they both said, then laughed because they had walked on each other's words.

"I'm sorry you go first…" Cas said to Emma.

Emma laughed and then started to cough.

Cas got up out of his seat to give Emma a pat on the back but when she coughed the next time she almost fell in his arms.

Emma was trying to clear her lungs of the coffee she inhaled, when she felt that helpful nudge from her aunt. *"Seriously…"* She thought.

Cas caught Emma up and taking her mug and putting it down on the side table, he helped raise her arms.

Emma felt foolish and she sent silent threats towards her aunt down in Boston. *"If I get a hold of you Aunty you will get it…"*

Emma took a deep breath and tried to smile, though she felt awfully awkward.

Cas rubbed Emma's back and smiled. "It's okay, it happens to the best of us. Really. I've had a lot of practice with little kids coming into the various stations I worked at and they inevitably inhale or choke on something."

Emma laughed and coughed at the same time. "Thanks, I think…"

She smiled at him and sat back down and took up her coffee mug. Holding it to her lips, she tried to think of something educated to say that would sound somewhat grown up. Nothing came to mind. *Boy I am batting a thousand… thanks Aunty!*

Cas knew when first meeting someone it could be awkward, but holding her seemed to put some ice on the situation. "So what do you bake for the Inns and B&Bs?" He watched as Emma became alive and animated, her eyes bright and hands moving as she talked.

"I love to bake. I bake whatever they need or want. I have been in the kitchen ever since I can remember. I helped with baking bread and buns when my mother baked. I started baking for my Aunt down in Boston when she had her, um, friends over… for tea. I went to school for business but finally surrendered myself to the fact I was happiest in the kitchen."

Cas sat back. "Not such a bad thing if you ask me."

Emma got up and took Cas's mug. "No, but it's hard not to sample. I have to exercise constantly."

Cas could picture her exercising and he could think of a couple exercises he would like do with her. He felt himself getting a boner so stood and pushed it down, following Emma back into Paul's kitchen.

"So you have a lot of customers?"

"Yes, I have more since the beginning of the summer. I can't complain but wish some days I had help. You know when something happens, as it did when we first met, it was a nightmare to catch up." *If only he knew what she did to catch up and have all her baking done. It was a lot of magic for sure.*

Cas took the mug of coffee offered and took her hand as they went back out onto the deck.

"Have you ever wanted to hire someone to help out?"

Emma nodded and put her mug down. "Yes, I just haven't had a chance to hire anyone. More than likely after this holiday I will. I just can't take the little time I have to train. They would have to be someone like my friend Kathy who already knows the ropes, but she teaches part-time."

Cas studied Emma, "How about on my days off I come over? Even on the days I work I could be here by six every evening. We could make up things in advance."

Emma smiled and felt like leaning over and kissing him on the cheek. If only the spell would hold. She didn't know how long it would hold but she needed all the help she could get.

She heard her Aunt clear her throat. "Have I ever let you down? You will be fine."

Emma smiled and stood up. "Sounds like a plan. Now I probably should go home and make up my shopping list to get done and then be ready for our date."

Cas stood up and took her mug. "I'll take care of that." He put it down and then wrapping an arm around her, he bent and kissed her lightly on the lips. He heard a little sigh and smiled against her lips. "I will see you at seven tonight."

Emma looked down and bit her bottom lip. Then looking back up, she saw a crooked grin on his face which made him even more handsome. She quickly stood on her tiptoes and kissed Cas back, this time wrapping her arms around his neck. She didn't feel any shocks or sparks. She let her mouth open to his. Cas kissing her back as his tongue slipped in. God, she got all kinds of visions and then her who-hah was getting warm and wet. She was in trouble even if the spell held.

Cas felt electrified kissing Emma. He felt like sparks could shoot off of him. He had never felt anything like it and they had only kissed. If they were to have sex, what was it gonna be like? That thought sent a chill up and down his spine that settled over his cock.

Emma knew better then to risk another kiss. She wanted to, looked up into Cas's face and thought, *what is he gonna look like if we are...*"Lordy!"

"What?" Cas asked, looking very puzzled.

Emma kissed his nose and moved back. "Nothing, just a little hot in here..."

Cas laughed. "Yeah, I'd say it is."

Emma tried to move away but Cas kept hold of her hand. She smiled and he pulled her gently back in.

"Dress comfortably," he said.

Emma laughed. "I always do."

As Cas watched Emma walk away he could picture her with nothing but a sexy bra and panties on.

Paul could see Cas watching Emma walk home. "She's a hard one to get hooked on."

Cas laughed and walked back in through the door from the balcony. "I wouldn't say that. I'd say I am already getting hooked on her."

Paul stood leaning against the counter. He watched his Lieutenant as he poured himself another mug of coffee. "Well you are the first in I'd say years that is getting hooked on Emma Brewster."

Cas smiled. "That's not a bad thing. It's been a while for me too so..." Cas looked over at his coworker and new friend. "I'd say it's new beginnings for the both of us."

Chapter 7

Emma was putting her supplies away when her phone rang. Picking up the phone, she saw it was her Aunt Ernestine. She pushed the button and answered. "I'm putting you on speaker phone Aunt Tiny."

Aunt Ernestine, or as Emma had always called her Aunty Tiny, sat in her Boston Back Bay home, looking into her tea cup. She had just picked it up after turning it upside down. "So dear, how was your party last night, meet any new men, or become better friends with anyone you have known?" She smiled as she heard Emma putting things away and mumbling something.

"Yes, I can hear you perfectly," Ernestine said.

"Aunty, How long does that spell last?"

Ernestine studied her cup. "It all depends dear. Once you have the one you think is the one for you, then the spell will slowly unwind and you will go back to normal. But by then it shouldn't be a problem. You shouldn't be setting things on fire because you will be with the one you are meant for and your body, soul and spirit will be used to him. The quirks of being a fire-starter are different with everyone. You, like your great grandmother have a thing for men. Since you were little, if you saw a cute boy, sparks shot from your fingertips. Your power is connected to fire. We are all fire-starters in our family but we are all different. Can you imagine if we all had the problem you did when it came to the opposite sex?" Ernestine laughed at that. Most of the women in the Brewster family were too hot to handle in all areas of their lives.

Emma giggled. She could see her having sex with sexy firefighter Cas and setting the bed afire. "Emma that isn't a funny scene." Ernestine studied her tea leaves some more and then smiled. She poured some more tea in another teacup. "Now tell me, where are you going for your date tonight?"

Emma put the last of her baking supplies away. "I'm not sure but I do know we are going out to dinner and then out to dance."

"Dancing is good. That should give you a chance to feel your way around, so to speak. Remember never quench your spirit. Sometimes the best times in life come from our powers when we aren't using them but they lay on the surface."

Emma was worried again. "But Aunty, I don't want to start fires up again every time I see him, never mind touching him." She had thoughts of them kissing and his hair getting singed and sparks shooting from her lips.

Aunt Ernestine sipped her tea. "There is nothing to worry about, dear. You and he will be fine tonight. Have faith and believe miracles can happen, he may be the one. Each one of us Brewster women have been given the right one, have faith and relax."

Emma sat down on the stool at her kitchen counter. "I will try." She let out a sigh.

"Good, now get yourself ready for that date and stop worrying." Ernestine pushed the button to her phone. She needed another cup of tea. If what she saw in her crystal earlier was truly going to happen, she needed to get to work.

* * * *

Emma was tearing her closet apart when she heard Kathy yelling from the stairs.

"I'm in here…"

Kathy could see things flying through the air as she climbed the stairs, since Emma's bedroom was at the top of the stairs it was easy to know who the room belonged to. When Emma was upset or agitated, things flew through the air.

"Ok sista, you need to take a deep breath and chill."

Emma looked over at Kathy, took a deep breath and all the clothes that had been flying around dropped right where they were.

"Well that's a fine mess you got us into, Ollie…" Kathy laughed as she started picking up the clothes that now lay in heaps. "You need one outfit, not enough to have a fashion show."

Emma plopped down on the bed. She held one of her sweaters to her chest. "What happens if what I pick doesn't make me look right? What if it makes me look fat?"

Kathy threw the armload of clothes down and stared at her best friend with an open mouth. "Since when have you ever looked fat? Just because you eat some of the stuff you bake, doesn't mean you're fat."

Emma looked down at her body. She had on a pair of skinny jeans and a royal blue corset over her signature peasant blouse." Look at me, my boobs about pop out of my corset. Doesn't that tell you I'm fat?"

Kathy jumped up. "And your point is with that question? You are beautiful. You look amazing in those corsets. With your ivory skin and perfect boobs you are the dream of many but no one has gotten near you. You need to keep your mystique up. Wear what you are used to. Don't make it easy, don't make it free." Kathy saw her friend's look. "I'm sorry, you really like him don't you?" She sat down on the bed with a thud.

Emma climbed up on the bed next to her best friend. "He kissed me last night and no sparks. I had visions of us doing... well you know what and the bed was afire. I know I am passable in the looks department."

Kathy was ready to hit her friend. She pushed her instead. "One you are not fat, two you are not passable in the looks department, you are so beautiful. I used to think who would want red hair? Then as we got older I saw all the guys checking you out and I noticed you got more looks than anyone else. Don't worry about looks or sparks or anything. Just be natural and yourself and he will be falling head over heels in love with you before you know it."

Emma laughed and lay back down among her clothes. "I'm not looking for love…" She saw Kathy making faces at her and knew she wasn't being true with even herself. "Ok, so maybe I want to fall in love. His kisses are amazing and I would love to have someone in my life, like him. I just hope I don't scare him away with my powers or my cats."

Kathy jumped up and pulled Emma to her feet. "Go take a shower. I will go make a pot of tea and when you get out I will do your hair and make up for you."

Emma looked at her best friend. "You really are a great friend."

Kathy smiled at her best friend. "I know."

Kathy hugged Emma. "Now go take a shower so I can put some make up on you and do something with your hair. It's standing on end."

Emma screamed and ran to the mirror. "Oh my god. I forgot about my hair."

Kathy started walking out of Emma's room. "Well shoot off some bolts in the shower. You need to get rid of all the extra power apparently stored up in your body."

Emma stood staring at her hair, pulling it down

and trying in vain to flatten it.

"I told you shoot off some bolts in the shower. That's the only thing that is going to work at this point. It's kinda like masturbating for witches with powers like yours," Kathy said with a laugh.

Kathy walked downstairs, leaving Emma standing staring at herself.

Emma stayed in front of the mirror for a few more minutes. She hoped between shooting off bolts in the shower and Kathy's way with hair, her hair would be tame tonight. She didn't need a freak show with her hair on a first date.

* * * *

Cas checked himself in the mirror and saw he looked okay. He had been looking over his clothes again and again and figured he might as well just go with what he was comfortable in. Jeans was his basic and he was comfortable in them. When he wasn't working he was in jeans. He had tossed different shirts around looking at them and finally settled on a cream colored sweater with a v-neck. Since he was well built, he filled out the sweater well. The cream color went with his brown eyes. His family always said he got the whole batch of chocolate when he was born due to the coloring of his eyes. It was due in fact that his mother was Italian and had fallen for an Irish boy from Southie.

Walking out of his bedroom, he looked around at his home and saw how sparse it all looked. He had signed the papers and it was indeed his house. What would he do, though, if he became involved with a lady who had her own place like Emma? Well, one thing at a time. He really liked her. She was sexy as all get out and she had the most amazing breasts that just begged to be touched and kissed.

She had taken his boner in hand and had been so sweet and sexy about it. He didn't want to necessarily get right into bed but it was nice to know he still worked. After being in *that* fire two years ago and getting so badly hurt he was afraid he would never be the same again. That had also been when he had started to feel like he was shooting off sparks from his fingers. Then last night kissing Emma, he felt electrified. Well he was going to go slow and see how it went.

* * * *

Midnight jumped up on the windowsill. He knew Emma was expecting *that human man* back. He had gotten a hint of his scent when he left and if only Emma could. She wasn't a cat or dog or vampire so she couldn't detect scents. Probably good thing. That man named Cas was excited. Well he was going to make sure he behaved himself. He would have a little talk with him before they went out.

Mica jumped onto the counter and looked at Emma as she did something to her face. She was spreading something on it. *What was that she called it?*

Emma was putting the finishing touches of her makeup on by adding a little lip-gloss, when she heard the doorbell ring. "Crap. I will be right there," she yelled. She saw Midnight jump off the windowsill. She didn't have a good feeling about her familiar. That possessed cat was up to no good.

She ran to the door. Midnight tripped her up. "Midnight! Behave yourself."

She opened the door and there stood Cas. She sucked in her breath. He looked amazing. The sweater he wore, probably cashmere, clung to all the right places on his chest. Showing his chest off just right. Emma was getting visions of pushing him against the wall, bringing his arms up so they were over his head and holding them there with a spell of silken ribbons, so he didn't know she was casting a spell. Then she would slowly kiss his chest, after she ripped the sweater off of course.

"Wow, you look great Cas." She hoped she didn't appear to be attacking him with her eyes.

She saw Midnight making a beeline for Cas so she bent and picked him up. "Why don't you just come in and I will be right with you."

Emma held Midnight, who fought in her arms to get free. "You had better behave yourself." She finally grabbed him by the scruff of the neck because that was the only way to hold him when he was about to change into something else. She put him in the bathroom and closed the door quickly. *"There, you can let yourself out after twenty minutes."*

Emma smiled as she walked back to the kitchen. She saw Cas sitting at the counter patting Mica. Mica was meowing up a storm. If only he knew what she was saying.

"I hope you know she is not loose, even though you see her dressed the way she is. Now she may act excited to see you, big boy, but you just rein in all that testosterone. She needs a real guy, someone who will understand her, not just a one night stand, as the humans call it. She may look like she wants a good time but what she wants and what she needs are two different things. And..."

Emma got just about all of Mica's rant and she was just started. She grabbed Cas's hand and pulled him to the door. "Come on, no sense in wasting the night. I want to dance."

Cas ran outside into the cool night behind Emma who seemed to be in a rush. He saw Emma had not brought a coat of any kind. It was one of those clear, cool nights and he knew she was going to be cold if she stayed like this outside for too long.

Cas pulled Emma to a stop. "What's the rush? It's not like we have to be to dinner till seven thirty. It's just here in Cadwell Harbor." Cas studied her and she seemed to be in a rush, for whatever reason. He pulled her in gently. She was cold and goose bumps stood out on her arms as well as her breasts that poked out of her jet black corset. He took off his leather coat and put it on her shoulders. "Here if you are in such a rush, use my leather jacket."

Emma let Cas put the jacket on her. "Thank you… I just didn't want the cats bothering you, I know they can be funny with new people."

Cas smiled and adjusted the coat. "I don't mind cats. They are their own animal and there is no explaining their behavior. Sometimes they are friendly and other times standoffish." He stood there and saw her rubbing her arms. "Come on, we can go to the bar and wait with a drink before our table is ready." He wrapped his arm around her to give her a bit of warmth and brought her to the passenger side of his truck. Opening the door he held her arm as she climbed up in. He saw she was visibly chilled so he hurried over to get in. Climbing in, he saw her rubbing her hands together so he turned on the truck and turned on the heater. "If you want, take my coat and go run in and get something more to wear, but you are welcome to wear my leather coat, since I am plenty warm with this sweater."

Emma felt foolish. She could have grabbed her leather coat too but had wanted to get Cas out and away from her demented cats. "I'm fine, if you are cold, just let me know. Once I warm up I will be okay but I just didn't want the cats attacking you."

She turned after buckling her seat belt so she was facing him more. She felt the blast of the heat and snuggled down in his coat. She felt his warmth and could smell him and a touch of his cologne. It was subtle, not overpowering. She got pictures going through her head but was jarred out of her thoughts. "I'm sorry I was daydreaming."

Cas could see she had left planet earth for a second. He was hoping he wasn't boring her already. "No, I was just asking if you have had much trouble with your neighbor before?"

Emma smiled ruefully. "Oh, Miss Crabtree... She and her ancestors have been a pain in our family's backside for years. She started, well long before I was born. Every year she complains and prowls. I think it's getting worse though. She has done some things that border on scary."

Cas drove down Bay Street. He spied a parking spot and pulled in. Turning towards Emma, he said ,"Well I hope you know the police should know about anything she does that you don't feel comfortable with."

Emma felt touched by his concern. "Oh I'm sure she is fine, just a little senile. I have heard our local retirement home is working on papers to get her in. I think it would be good for her since she doesn't have any family to speak of."

Cas saw Emma must have warmed up since she

wasn't shivering any more. The soft, street light coming in the windshield made her look ravishing. She was creamy perfection in a black leather corset and tight jeans. Her lips were red, and her makeup was soft, not bold. Her red hair fell in soft waves on her shoulders. He wanted to bury himself in her breasts and just camp out there awhile.

"Cas…" Emma saw he was really studying her. *Maybe I should have worn the sweater…*

Cas jumped to the sound of his name. "Sorry, just thinking about you being cold. You can keep my jacket on all night."

He got out and walked around to her side of her truck. Opening up her door he took her hand and helped her down. Her breasts jiggled a little. He was really gonna need to rein it in. He could feel his cock reacting to the sight of her. The last thing he wanted her to think was he was just going out with her for a tasty treat.

Wrapping a protective arm around her, they walked in the door and up to the hostess station.

The hostess came out from the bar area and saw Emma Brewster with the hunky new firefighter. God, how did she land him? She looked at Emma, saw her in one of her corsets. Why she wears those corsets, like she was trying to flaunt her boobs. Well probably trying to take away any notice to her red hair.

"Hey Emma, wow I didn't know you were in that reservation with Mr. O' Halloran." Tammy smiled sweetly at Cas. "If you two can take a seat at the bar I will have your server come get you when your table is ready."

Cas kept his arm around Emma. He saw Emma giving the hostess *a look*.

Emma heard all Tammy's thoughts. What a bitch, and she thinks she is pretty. She would be if she wasn't always putting people down. But she didn't expect her to change. They had known each other since they were little and the only thing Tammy was good for was being consistent and that was being a bitch.

"Hey Tammy, yes, Cas and I met at the bagel shop first and then a couple fire calls at my house."

Tammy pointed towards the bar. "Well, find a seat at the bar and we will have your table ready soon."

As Tammy walked away, Emma twisted her finger in her direction. Tammy stepped and then went flying, landed on her face and swore, which brought stares from all the patrons in the restaurant. She jumped up and tried to rearrange her skirt and blouse which had a nice smudge across her chest. Emma gave her a *look* before she was steered towards the bar by Cas.

Emma sat on the bar stool, she felt the warmth of the fire that blazed in the big fireplace behind them. She leaned into Cas as he whispered in her ear.

"I reserved the table by the fireplace." Emma smiled at him. His eyes were so warm and inviting.

Boy I better stop those thoughts…

Cas saw the bartender looking at Emma's breasts. He gave him the *look* and saw him look away for a fraction of a second and then clear his throat.

Emma looked up at the bartender and saw it was Tammy's boyfriend from high school, Billy Cobb. He had shown interest in Tammy after he had been turned down by herself. She had just said she didn't think it would work out. Emma remembered all too well making out in his truck. Emma had opened her eyes and could see things flying around the cab. So she had slapped him when he touched her boob and said she wanted to go home.

"Hey Emma…"

Emma smiled. "Hey Billy… I will have a club soda with lime and a shot of tequila…" She saw his eyes pop open and then a smile spread on his face.

Cas couldn't believe Emma was ordering a shot of tequila.

Emma smiled sweetly over at Cas. "To warm me up and take the edge off. Don't worry, I won't get drunk on it."

Cas shrugged his shoulders. "Make that the same for me, but give us the best."

Billy grabbed the bottle down and showed it to Cas.

"Yup, that will do."

Tammy came up to Emma and hunky firefighter. "Your table is ready. Billy if they have drinks, just bring them over to them, here." She pointed to their table that was right behind them.

Cas got down and let Emma go first. They sat and Emma took off Cas's leather coat.

"I think I will be fine, for now."

Billy brought over the drinks and smiled at Emma, saw Cas's look, turned and left quickly.

Cas saw the fire light make Emma's eyes and hair come alive. Her eyes gave off sparks and her hair glowed. While he watched her he saw her take a deep breath.

Emma felt all the fear flow out of her. Her aunt must have placed another spell on her to relax because a half an hour ago she was feeling so scared and frigid, which would have been a good way to describe her. Now she felt carefree.

Picking up her shot she looked over at Cas. She knew she must look like a nymph. "To tonight..." she downed it with one gulp. She felt the tequila spread down through her body. Along with that was the warmth it gave. She saw Cas smile.

"To tonight..." Cas took the tequila in one shot and then put his shot glass down.

Emma saw Cas's eyes light up. It was like there was a spark or something.

"So Cas tell me why you came to Cadwell Harbor of all places?"

Cas smiled and took one menu and gave it to Emma. "I will tell you, but let's get our food ordered first."

Emma took the menu. She always had a healthy appetite but she was going to cut back tonight.

She saw what she wanted and waited for Cas.

Cas glanced up, saw Emma's face all aglow. Her eyes were really big pools of light.

"How about we split an appetizer?"

Emma nodded. "Sure…"

Cas looked at the menu again and saw the calamari. "How about calamari?"

Emma was fine with that. "Sure."

They waited and finally their waitress came over. She looked first at Emma.

Emma had seen a couple things she liked, but she figured she knew what she would get. "Pan seared scallops…" She said to the waitress.

"Wow, I was going to get that myself. Do you mind if I get that too?" Cas asked.

Emma laughed. "No, that's fine… it's funny you and I wanting the same thing."

They each took a sip of their club sodas and then sat with awkward silence between them.

Cas took another sip and then a deep breath. "Okay, so I decided on Cadwell Harbor because I saw the opening in the magazine we had at our station. I figured since I always wanted to live in Maine someday this was a chance. There is a bigger, better chance of advancement if I am here too."

Cas watched Emma and the range of emotions on

her face. She really was so beautiful. "So tell me more about yourself."

Emma smiled, took another sip of her water. "Ok, I love to bake, eat what I have baked. Hate exercise but do run. I love antiques, horses, have one boarded at a farm outside of town. I have one really good friend, Kathy. I have two wacky cats, but you know that." She saw his smile and she realized he had a dimple. When she stared at him more she saw the dimple deepen and another appeared on the other cheek. "You have dimples…"

Cas laughed and took the last swallow of his club soda. "Yes… I wasn't happy about them when I was younger because my Italian grandmother was always pinching me on the cheeks and saying I was so cute. I thought with all her pinching my cheeks, she gave them to me. It wasn't until I was older that I finally realized they helped catch girls."

Emma was feeling the tequila and was really relaxed. Their waitress came, bringing them their calamari and she asked for two more club sodas with lime.

"I will take another club soda…" Cas said.

"Emma leaned over to him, I ordered one for you too, not two for me."

Cas could feel the tequila and was smiling from ear to ear. He hoped he didn't look like an idiot. "Thank you."

Aunt Ernestine watched what was going on in the

crystal. Her friend peeked over her shoulder. "You better back off on them being relaxed or they will be falling asleep and won't be awake to go dancing."

Ernestine took a sip of her spiked tea. "I know Violet, let me take care of them and we can shut things down for tonight."

Ernestine spoke softly into the crystal, whispering things that were for the crystal only. She smiled "So it be done…"

Emma jumped and saw Cas jump too. *God what are you up to Aunty?* She heard nothing so figured she had walked away from her crystal.

They sat eating the calamari, laughing at stories the other told. By the time their dinners arrived Emma felt like she had known Cas all her life.

Cas could see a transformation in Emma. She wasn't shy or aloof any longer. She sparkled and her eyes were as bright as emeralds. She had the same wicked sense of humor he did.

"You know I don't know when I have enjoyed myself so much as I have with you, Emma."

Emma looked up and pushed a stray crumb into her mouth from her piece of pie. Then she watched as Cas reached over and gently wiped another stray crumb from the side of her mouth. Then wonder of wonders, he wiped one off her bottom lip. She had to fight back the urge to either kiss his finger, suck on it or lick it. She started getting visions as she let her tongue lick where his finger just left. She felt like lust had hit her with a freight train and she wanted to be hit a few more times. Her who hah was going right to melt down mode with the touch of his finger to her lip. Her panties were going to be wet and she hadn't even cum yet.

Cas looked up and saw their waitress. He gave her his card without even looking at the bill. Took the slips, signed one, pocketed the other and pulled Emma to her feet. He wrapped his leather coat around her shoulders. Then taking her hand, he led her outside and into the night and to his truck. Unlocking his truck and opening the door, he turned and Emma dove at him

Emma had a feeling of lust come over her and she didn't know what to do with it. When in doubt, attack the hunky man you are with. She caught his face and pushed herself into him. Felt his lips kissing her back and then she was on fire and she was sure they were both going to go up in flames. His lips were seeking hers as much as she was attacking his. His mouth left her lips and as he kissed his way from her chin to her neck. She sent out a silent prayer to the Goddess and her aunt to save them from the fire that she was sure was erupting all around them.

"Oh my god Emma, I don't want you to think…"

Emma pushed him back to his seat. "I'm not thinking right now, Cas, if you haven't noticed." She kissed him again and let her hands do some walking. She was making her way down his neck when Cas spun her around and had her up in his truck quick.

"Push over, we aren't taking this here anymore. We need to decide, do we go dancing or go have…"

Emma was back on his lap and kissing him hard. *When was the last time I had sex?* She thought, she couldn't remember and her best toys didn't count so she knew this was going to be a hot time in the old town tonight.

"No dancing…" she said in a breathless reply.

Cas saw her breasts peeking out of her corset and his leather jacket. He had to touch his face to them. Dipping his face onto her breasts, he felt the perfection of her pert breasts and knew. "No dancing… My place or yours?"

Emma was climbing off his lap. "Yours, my cats wouldn't behave tonight if they tried…"

Cas started up the truck and had them up the street and heading out to the lake and his new house.

Pulling in next to his house, Cas took a deep breath. He leaned across Emma and opened the glove box. Grabbed the bag from the pharmacy, he saw Emma's questioning look. "I bought them today for…" saw her smile. "For just in case…"

He took her hand and pulled her out. He had them up to the door and in the house quickly. He pulled her into the living room and pushed her down onto the couch. Kissing her, he then stood up. "Hold that thought while I build a fire. If you want go to the bathroom, there is a linen closet right next to the door.

Get a blanket or two..." He turned and went to the fireplace and started laying kindling down and lighting it up. Emma watched for a second and went to the bathroom. She found the blankets and as she came walking back she wiggled her finger in front of the fire. It flared and took off.

She dropped the blankets on the floor and started spreading them out. As she bent to fix the last corner she felt Cas behind her. She arched into him and felt him take ahold of her, kissing her back. She turned into his arms and felt his strong arms around her, gathering her up, kissing her lips, her chin and then her neck.

"Do you mind if I just worship your..."

He let his finger stray over them and she giggled.

"Mmm, as long as you want," she said.

He lay her down on the blankets. Emma lay watching Cas as he studied her in the firelight.

"You're beautiful, Emma..."

She arched and purred like a cat would have but she wanted to be touched. So she started to unhook her corset and watched him as he watched her hands and as more skin appeared. She stretched and moaned because she could almost feel his touch. He leaned in as the last hook was released and her breasts were set free. As he buried his face in between her breasts she gently held his head there till he lifted up his face. There was a smile on it and his dimples showed. Then he bent and took one of her nipples in his mouth, letting his tongue swirl around it, gently sucking on it till Emma thought she would go crazy with the need to have him in her.

Cas had to touch her, had to taste every inch of her. He let his hand find her jeans and as she moved with him, he teased one nipple and then the other. He found his hand exploring in her jeans. He found her and found she was all natural. "Good, you aren't clean shaven…"

Emma had thought about shaving but thought what was the likelihood of them doing anything tonight?

"I'm glad…" he said against her neck. He was kissing her breasts again, pulling her jeans off and about to go down on her when the tones went off.

Emma jumped. "What the fuck is that?" She asked as Cas sat up and waited for more.

Cas listened to different tones going off and knew this meant a structure fire.

"Cadwell Fire, Ducktrap fire, Cadwell EMS…confirmed structure fire at 66 Magnolia Street…

Emma looked at Cas as he jumped up.

"That's my house…"

Cas felt awful. "It's okay maybe it's nothing, maybe something small."

Emma jumped up grabbing her corset. She tried to get it back on but it was hopeless. Her fingers were all thumbs.

Cas ran to his room and came back, giving Emma a tee shirt. Here, wear this."

She slipped it on and then her jeans, then they ran outside to his truck. She climbed up in as Cas got in and started up his truck. He flipped on a switch and red lights lit the night up. Emma watched as he got on his portable radio.

"Cadwell dispatch, this is car 3… en-route to the scene, ETA 5 minutes."

Emma was crying. "What could have happened? I never leave anything on." She looked out the window at the black landscape and the occasional house and sent a silent prayer up to the Goddess to save her cats.

Cas took Emma's hand and gave it a squeeze. "It will be okay. The cats are fine, they have an ability to escape."

Cadwell Dispatch, to Car 3. We have word from the RP… Paul…

Emma sat up, "Paul is there?"

Cadwell Car 1, on scene, two story, wood frame construction, single family dwelling. Hold all mutual aid companies and Cadwell Engine 1 come in cold."

Cas pulled over and took Emma in his arms. "See I told you not to worry…" He pulled back and saw her face, saw tears running down her face, saw her makeup smudged. He kissed her nose and then her lips. Then pulling away, he looked in his side mirror and pulled back out onto the Turnpike Drive. He held her hand until they arrived at her house, parking behind Engine 1. She jumped out and was running up her lawn over hoses.

Emma didn't care who was there or what they saw. She was just about to run in the house when she saw on the ground a pink curler. She stopped mid-stride and bent over and picked it up.

Cas was right behind her. "What did you find?" He took the curler out of her hand and looked at it closely.

"You don't wear curlers do you?" He knew the answer before any words left his lips. He saw the grey hair caught in the curler.

Emma was madder than she had ever been. "And she calls me a witch... that mean old bitch." she started thinking of things she could do to her but remembered with her power came a responsibility to use it carefully. She pushed her thoughts away. She felt Cas's hand in hers as she went through the door. She saw the smoke in the air coming from the barn. She saw first Midnight and then Mica come running up to her, meowing up a storm.

"We don't know what happened, it was smoky all of a sudden, smelt like something put on the grill."

Emma picked up her cats to hug them. They worked their way out of her arms.

"Fluid..." Mica said quickly to Emma.

Mica jumped down and snaked around Cas's legs. *"Hey handsome, come with me I will show you..."*

Cas looked down and could see Emma's cat Mica

seemed to be wanting attention with the way she was meowing. He picked her up but she climbed right out of his arms.

Cas watched the cats as they kept up meowing. "Do you suppose they are trying to tell us something?"

Emma was getting everything the cats were saying. With the curler in her hand and the cats telling her about the fluid she knew.

"Come on. Let's go in the barn." She pulled his hand.

Chapter 8

Ernestine jumped up from the smoke smell swirling around her nose. Climbing out of bed she stood waiting. Why had she smelled smoke? *Oh no… did my spell not work or did it backfire?*

Ernestine grabbed her silk robe and wrapped it around her body. She then ran out of her room and down the hall to the stairs. She ran down them quicker than she had in years. She ran into the parlor and to her crystal which was better than any computer or cell phone. She uncovered it and waved her hand over it. There, she could see smoke, she could see bodies moving but couldn't see them yet. "Damn, what went wrong?" Then she saw and knew. "Double damn… that old witch needs to be put away!"

* * * *

Emma watched as Cas and his Chief poked around things in the barn. Paul backed up with a hose and, putting it down, looked at what they had found. A clump of pink curlers and a bottle of lighter fluid, all melted together at the scene of where the fire must have started.

"Well if that don't beat all," The Chief said as he studied the mass of burned and melted plastic. The scent of melted plastic and lighter fluid was strongest where they stood.

"She always gets worse this time of year Chief," Emma said as she touched the mass with her toe. She pulled the tee shirt she had on around her more and shivered. Paul saw and shucked off his coat and gave it to her to put on. Cas saw the gesture, saw Emma trying to handle the big turnout coat and he took it from her small hands and helped her with it. He picked up her chin. "Do you want to go in and make some tea? This is bound to be a shock and we won't be here for long. The chief will close off the area and have the arson squad come in the morning."

Emma nodded. She realized how close she came to losing her beloved cats. "Yes, I will go make some tea and coffee. Bring everyone in when you are finished." She stood on her tiptoes and kissed him lightly on the lips and walked back in through the carriage house that attached to the house.

Paul looked at his Lieutenant. "So have things changed?"

Cas looked over at Paul. "We are friends. If it goes to the next level I will let you know, since you were the one to introduce us officially."

Paul nodded. "Got ya."

The Chief walked in with yellow tape and some poles. "Here, stake this area off. Anything that can be used as evidence we want this whole place marked off. Cas, tell Emma not to come out here."

Cas nodded his head. "Yes Chief." He stood

staring at the melted mass of plastic. A blend of colors, pink and white. Why would that woman want to do that to Emma? Well we don't know for certain but it sure does look like old Miss Crabtree set it.

He was jarred out of his thoughts. "Hey Lieutenant, you going in for coffee?"

Cas looked up. "Yes, be right there."

He walked over to his Chief who was wiping his hands on a rag he had. "Chief, what's the history behind these two families?"

Chief didn't want to lose his best prospects for him retiring finally. But he didn't want to hand over the reins if he had an arsonist on the loose, even if it was Miss Crabtree.

"Let's just say it goes back generations."

Cas was trying to wrap himself around the whole part of Miss Crabtree's accusations against Emma and her family.

"It's never been this bad. Like Emma said, it always seems to get worse this time of year. It always starts with the block BBQ party and spirals till Halloween. We have to have police stationed around her house."

"Miss Crabtree's or Emma's?"

Chief put his portable away in his truck. "Both, actually. We have police around Emma's to keep her safe and around Miss Crabtree's to keep her in her house for the 24 hours leading up and until November first. It's become a part of the whole celebration and the tax payers of Cadwell Harbor started a fund a few years back to help pay for extra police presence. Even Emma's aunt down in Boston has a fundraiser in Boston and Salem has one too, to help defray with the cost. So that's how we keep everyone safe. I have heard they are trying to get her into Pleasant Hill, which is the retirement facility here that has cottages and a nursing facility for those needing around the clock care."

Cas started walking alongside his Chief as they walked to the porch that was on the side of Emma's house. He held the door for his Chief as they walked in. "Do you think we can get the old biddy in before this gets worse?"

His Chief shook his head. "I don't know. I'm not a cop and don't know for certain she set it, but with the evidence you gave us that Emma found and what we found at the burn scene it shouldn't be too hard. The State Fire Marshal will be here first thing in the morning to go over the scene. So just don't say anything to Emma or anyone…"

Cas nodded his head. "I won't."

They sat around the table eating brownies and drinking coffee. Finally the Chief bid everyone a good night and then Paul smiled and left.

Cas glanced up at the wall clock, saw it was just after midnight. He saw the cats walk through the kitchen like they didn't even exist. He got up and followed Emma to the sink. She was putting the dishes in her dishwasher. He came up behind her and wrapped his arms around her. Felt her stand frozen for a moment and then meld herself to him. Heard her sigh. He took her and turned her into him. Gathering her face in his hands he kissed her slow and long. Letting his lips find hers, and his tongue tasting her. Found the taste of chocolate and coffee an aphrodisiac. He wanted to taste all of her. He reached and turned off the light over the sink. Except for the light over the table, they stood in the dark.

Emma reached over her head and clapped her hands. The light went off. Seeing Cas's questioning glance. "I have the *Clap On*, a joke gift from Kathy."

She was shushed quiet with Cas's lips, who wanted nothing but to kiss her at this moment. He wanted to stay right here and make out till it got too much and he couldn't stand.

He let his lips kiss her lips, her cheeks, her chin. She had an adorable chin. When he reached her neck she arched into him and he felt his cock react. He felt her hand find him and he thought he was going to cum in an instant. God, he hoped he could last a while, but it had been a long time.

He felt her get hotter and then he felt his body start to heat up. He felt like a shock went through his body and landed on his cock. He had never felt anything like this before.

He lets his hands go from her face down her arms. Then lifting his tee that she wore, her breasts were in his hands and she was moving in a rhythm to his movements. As his lips made their way slowly down her neck, she was moving and grinding into him, sighing and moaning in turn. The whole combination was too much. He scooped her up. "Which way?"

Emma was kissing his neck. "Straight up the stairs." He was taking them two at a time because Emma was light as a feather. He saw the door and was in her room. Felt her reach to slam the door shut.

Emma was hoping neither Mika nor Midnight were anywhere in this room. She would strangle them with her own hands if they did anything to interrupt this time.

She saw Cas's face in the streetlight that shown in her room. She kissed his cheek and then his lips as he caught her lips.

Laying her down on her bed he braced both arms around her, bending he kissed her more. He couldn't get enough of her lips, but knew he needed to text his Chief. Standing back up, he took his phone out of his pocket. "I'm texting Chief to let him know unless it's another structure fire I am off duty till morning."

He took his phone and with shaking hands found his Chief's number and sent him a quick text. Then taking that and his pager, he put them on Emma's bedside stand. Then he reached into his other pocket and pulled a handful of condoms out. Saw Emma smile. "I was a boy scout. I always come prepared."

He was down on top of Emma, quickly gathering

her up and kissing her hard, feeling her body react to him. "First time might be quick, but it's only because it's been a while... not because of you Emma." He kissed her again and felt her small hands holding his face tenderly as he kissed her. Then he felt her hands skimming over his arms. She was whispering things that he didn't quite get but it sounded so seductive. His body reacted to her hands and her lips. Then she was pushing him to his side and she was up on her knees, taking off his tee and stretching like a contented cat. Then she was working her hands and lips down his body. She had his tee balled up in her hand and was kissing his stomach, letting her tongue work its way around his inny. He was in heaven. Then she was unsnapping his jeans and he thought he was going to explode with her touch and kisses as she worked her way down. She was teasing him, kissing his legs as she pulled his jeans down. Then she kissed around his boxers and he thought, *yup I'm gonna cum before she even touches me...*

He jumped as she pulled his boxers down, then she finally came in contact with him.

Emma looked up and saw Cas arch as she touched him. She was being bold and only knew this came with the spell her aunt had placed on her to relax and not be frigid. She was enjoying this so much, she wanted this and him so much. When she took ahold of him in her mouth she let her tongue swirl around his tip till she tasted a bit of him and heard his moan.

Then he was moving and had her on her back and it was her turn.

Emma was on fire. She was sure he would notice and if he did he would leave and never return. She saw his eyes but saw no reflection of flames in his eyes. All she saw was the heat and lust that he felt, just like her.

"I need to taste you Emma. I hope you don't mind, then I need to be in you." He didn't let her say a thing, he was spreading her legs and dipping his face in. He knew the instant he got her scent and let his tongue lick into her that he was home. He was the homing pigeon and this was his home. He licked into her and felt her buck. He heard her say 'yes', and then she was holding his head tightly as she moved while he licked her over and over again.

Emma could feel all the emotions of the day and the feelings of lust and longing come to a pinpoint. She wanted to take in every feeling but it was too quick, she was going to let go. She tried getting up on her elbows so she could watch him. She saw his eyes once and then he was pushing her down and she was gone. She shattered into a million sparks all at once while she let go.

He knew now or never. He let her slow down and then he was reaching for a condom and putting it on. He was spreading her legs and slipping in her, finding her hot, very wet and very tight. Looking down into her face, he saw her smile.

"You're beautiful Emma." He took her lips and kissed her. She took his tongue and sucked on it as they kissed and he started the slow movements of loving her completely. He felt her hands on his butt cheeks, pulling him in and squeezing his ass as he thrust in her again and again.

"That's it Cas, like that… like…"

Cas was going to cum, he felt her move with him and knew neither of them were going to last. He saw her one last time as he felt himself about to explode. Heard her say his name and then as she screamed his name he let go.

Chapter 9

As Cas let his heart come back to a normal heartbeat, he pulled Emma into the crook of his arm. Kissing the top of Emma's head, he felt her small hands playing with his chest hair and felt her lips kissing his chest. Then she was up on her knees.

Emma wanted a shower and she wanted to wash him. "Come on, come with me and let's take a shower."

Emma got the water going, pulled out two large towels and then a new bar of soap. She turned and saw Cas studying her. She saw his slow, sexy smile spread on his face, his dimples really showing up. She climbed into the tub and pulled him in. They closed the curtain and she stood under the water, letting it soak her. She watched as Cas got closer and pulled her in. Capturing her face in his calloused hands, he kissed her gently at first then she felt his need and his kisses becoming more urgent. His hands were all over her, touching her, mapping her body.

Cas had her breasts in his hands, bending, catching one nipple and then the other in his mouth. Each time he sucked on a nipple she arched into him, moans escaping her lips. "I'm mapping out your body, learning the little spots that when I touch or kiss them, it turns you on."

Emma was letting his mouth and the water do it's

magic. She felt no flames erupting from her so knew whatever spell her aunt had placed on her, it was safe to say they were okay. She moaned and caught some of the water in her mouth.

Cas picked up the soap and started to lather Emma's body up. He paid careful attention to her breasts. God, he could worship her breasts, but then there were her curves. He soaped her up and then let his hands work like a facecloth as he moved the suds around. Then he soaped up his hand again as he watched her face, he let his hand go between her legs while finding her clit and lips. He saw her eyes close and her fingernails dug into his shoulders. He didn't want to her cum so he took his hand away and saw her pout. He kissed her lips and she bit down on his bottom lip gently. Turning her around he soaped up her adorable fanny. Then, bending her over, he took his hardened cock and took her all over again. She moaned and grabbed the tub's faucet. He let his head go back and felt water go in his mouth. Spitting it out, "Oh god Emma, you are so tight. You wrap around me like a glove." He felt his brain go to mush as he took her hips and moved her back and forth as his cock plunged into her harder and harder. He heard her incoherent words and knew she was close. He was trying to stay with the moment but feeling her pussy get tighter and tighter only brought him closer to where he wanted to be.

Emma had only been with two men and Cas was

her second. She had never had sex in a shower and she never knew it could be so good. She thought she wouldn't have another orgasm but she was about ready to let go again. She grabbed one of his thighs as she held onto the faucet with the other hand. She knew she was going to scream so she stuffed her hand in her mouth so not to bring the cats running. She saw nothing but white as her mind and body went over the edge again.

Cas saw her stuff her hand in her mouth. He had been letting his body go with the feeling as he said and uttered things he had never said before. This was it. He felt her pussy clamp down on him and he knew he better exit or take the chance of spilling into her since he didn't have a condom on. He pulled out, heard her whimper as he exploded all over her back. Pulling her in hard he rocked the two of them in their orgasms.

* * * *

Emma wrapped her arms around his neck as they stood under the water, her head resting on his chest. "Will you stay the night?"

Cas smiled as he kissed her head. "Wild horses couldn't drag me away from you."

They washed each other and then got out. Cas wrapped a towel around his hips, then started to towel dry Emma. Then hanging the towel, he scooped her up and brought her back into her bedroom. Placing her down, he took his towel and quickly dried his body and then let the towel fall. Climbing into her bed, he caught up her body and pulled her into a spoon shape hug. Pulling covers over them, he closed his eyes and sighed. He felt like he was home.

* * * *

Midnight stood up on his hind legs and got the doorknob in his paws. He almost had it opened when the knob slipped. *"Drat... what can I change myself into that would open the door"?*

Mika stood looking at the problem. Midnight thought he was the only one with the brains. She was hungry and Emma was sleeping far too late. She always called them her flying monkeys... *"I have it... a monkey, a flying monkey."*

Midnight looked over at his fellow familiar and thought, she does have brains after all. He smiled at her, turned and went to the other end of the hallway. He started walking slowly and by the time he got up to Mika had changed.

"Well, you certainly look the part of her evil flying monkey..." Mika laughed.

Midnight walked to the bathroom and, jumping up on the sink, he could see that he had indeed changed into a flying monkey.

"Just make sure you change before you let them

see you… You may do some damage if he sees you." Mika said.

Midnight turned and gave Mika one of his looks. *"What do you take me for? Of course I will change, once I am in there."*

He jumped down and headed back to Emma's bedroom door. He grasped the door and loved the feeling of the knob in his hands. *"This wasn't bad… it would be nice to be more like a human… maybe I will stay this way for a while."*

Mika looked at Midnight like he was nuts. *"You can't… it's one thing to be her familiar, as a cat or in other forms when she is around alone but you know she would have a fit if we appeared like anything else than what we are supposed to be."*

Midnight gave her a contemptuous look and pushed the door open.

They both stood there and saw the bed move.

Mika swatted at Midnight. *"Come back, you fool. She will kill us if he finds out about her and us before she wants him to."*

Midnight swished his monkey tail and made a sound that sounded like *tsk, tsk, tsk.*

Turning over Cas felt Emma turn with him. They had slept in the spoon form all night. He had been conscious of their movements all night, enjoying the feel of her body molded to his. He laid there for a few minutes and then heard one of the cats meow. He lazily opened his eyes and saw the Torti and she was meowing up a storm. Then he caught site of a ... flying monkey? He lay there. Both Mika and the flying monkey stood where they were, frozen. He blinked his eyes and then figured he was still sleeping. *What the hell. I am probably dreaming of a flying monkey cause of Old Miss Crabtree and her accusations of Emma being a witch...* he sighed and turned his back and felt Emma turn back so she nestled herself right back into him. He could sleep like this forever if Emma was at his side.

Mika swatted Midnight again. *"Do you see how close you came... you will ruin it for her. Change back right now."*

Midnight turned his head away from Mika. *What a spoil sport.* *"I will change when I am good and ready."*

Emma slowly started to wake. The room was awash with the morning light. She felt Cas's arm over her. She smiled. Then she heard what must have woken her. Her cats were meowing and they were in her room. Then her brain came awake. She had shut the door, how did they get in?

She moved Cas's arm and slowly sat up. She almost screamed. There on her bed was Midnight, all black and as a flying monkey. Mika was next to him admonishing him. She threw out her arm and changed him back into a cat.

"Midnight Brewster, keep it up and you won't be

my familiar any more… Now listen to Mika and get out!"

Midnight looked at his paw, which was a cat's paw again. He jumped down in disgust. *"I can never have any fun."*

He walked out of the room.

Mika looked at her mistress. *"I am sorry, Emma."*

Emma reached and patted her cat. "It's okay. Just keep an eye on him."

Emma felt eyes on her. She turned and saw Cas awake and he had a sexy smile on his face. She saw his dimples and she fell on him, kissing him, laughing as his hands found her and pulled her in with a kiss that promised so much more.

Cas sat at the counter while Emma pulled sticky buns out of the oven. She had dough rising overnight so when they came downstairs she had whipped them up so fast. By the time he was done with his third cup of coffee and reading the sports section in the newspaper, they were coming out of the oven. Filling the kitchen with an intoxicating aroma.

Emma smiled over at Cas. "Would you like some?"

Cas was up and around the counter in a couple steps. "Since you didn't make clear what you were offering. I can think of more than one thing I would like. I want you first and I want to spread cream or icing all over your body." He kissed her and let his tongue taste her sweetness. He had her so many times last night and he was just finding out how much he wanted her more and more. He felt her touching him and he felt the heat spread through his body, just like an electric current. He was electrified as her touch spread over his body. He felt alive and gloried in the feeling that as spreading with the lust. He pulled away and saw her unfocused look and smiled. She looked like he felt. He pushed her hair to the side and caught her neck in a kiss and gently nipped on her ivory skin. Then he felt her pushing his boxers down as she lifted her leg over his hip. She said one word.

"Now…"

He moaned as he kissed her, filling her with himself. Her moans and whimpers fueled his need to be in her more. She had cast a spell over him and he would gladly stay with her for the rest of his days if he could just have her like this and all the ways they had made love throughout the night.

Chapter 10

Emma was back home from deliveries and found the local florist van parked in her driveway. It was the third time this week she had received flowers.

The woman from the flower shop had a smile on her face. "It appears you have an admirer, Emma."

Emma smiled and took the small vase. She noticed it wasn't the usual one from the florist but from the looks an antique and a white clear hobnob vase at that. In it were three crimson roses. She felt a current run through her, she felt warm and cared for. What was he saying with the three roses? Since they were crimson, that usually signified love.

Sally from the florist shop smiled at Emma. She had always like Emma. "He came in to the shop with that vase, said he had found it at the antique shop in town. He wanted something different for you because you weren't like any woman he had ever seen or known."

Emma buried her nose in the roses and inhaled the slight fragrance. She looked up at Sally's face. "He is pretty special."

Sally smiled. "Well it's obvious he has a thing for you. Maybe he will be the first guy to get a Brewster woman who isn't from Harvard."

Emma smiled. "Actually he is from Harvard, as in Harvard, Massachusetts. He only moved to Boston when he went to college."

Sally smiled. "Well you go, girl! It's about time you got a man."

Emma smiled as she walked into the house with her roses. She saw Midnight sleeping on his bed in the big kitchen window. She saw him open one eye and then close it as quickly as it opened. Mika, on the other hand, jumped down from her perch and wrapped herself around her ankles.

"Emma, another... this is three... do you think he loves you? Do you think he will be the one?"

Emma stood there and listened to Mika's meows. She was in another world when Cas arrived. She tried to stay centered when he wasn't. But the flowers and now the roses were making her think and feel things she had never felt before for anyone other than her parents and that was a different love. She was afraid her powers were going to scare him away. She bent and patted Mika. *"What do I do? What if I am falling in love?"*

Mika looked up at her mistress and tried to wrap around her ankle more. That way she could hear her thoughts better. Maybe she, as a familiar in training could help if she could feel what it was like to be a human witch and have those things called love. *"What is love?"*

"Love, I think it's how I am feeling, Mika."

Cas had tiptoed into Emma's house and had seen Emma studying the roses. He had sent that silent message in hopes she wouldn't hold it against him when he told her how he was feeling. They had been dating for two weeks and in two days it was Halloween. He was going to propose to her. He knew it was quick but he had never known feelings like he had now.

He pulled her in and kissed her back as she was bent over patting her cat. "It's what I am feeling for a certain witchy baker who has wrapped herself around my heart."

Emma stood and turned into Cas's arms. She hoped to god she hadn't said anything to let him know she and Mika were communicating. She drew herself back and smiled. "I have fallen for you Cas."

Cas scooped up Emma till her feet were off the floor. "I love you, Emma Brewster. You were too hot to handle at first, all hot and twitchy like you were going to catch afire…"

Emma smiled. If only you knew… if only I could figure out how to tell you.

"Just tell him. What's the worst he can do but leave you… that would be a welcome change. Midnight said as he lazily stretched.

Mika jumped up into Midnight's face and yowled and spat at Midnight.

Cas smiled as he kissed Emma's nose. "It seems your cats are having a spat."

Emma pulled Cas in tight. She let his arms wrap around her. She needed to be honest and tell him. She would just need an opening. Her familiars fighting over this subject was not good. Midnight became explosive when he was like this.

"You really love me? Even with my cats?" she said against Cas's chest as he hugged her and kissed her head.

Cas pulled away from Emma and looked at her. "Yes, even with your cats. I fell in love with the whole package... you, the cats and the crazy baking schedule which matches mine at the fire department. I think we are a great match." He picked up her chin and smiled at her. "I'd like to figure out a living arrangement for us."

Midnight had heard enough. Living arrangements? He looked at Emma's back as she was being hugged by that firefighter and figured he would take care of things all on his own. What better way than to show *that Cas fellow* about Emma's little secret. He looked over at Mika and smiled an evil smile. *"Watch this..."*

Mika opened her mouth in protest but nothing came out, but when it did it was a very loud yowl.

Emma was kissing Cas when she heard the warning yowl. She sent up a silent message to her aunt, who always had an open line to her going. Then she sent a silent message to the Goddess. She didn't dare look but didn't dare not look.

"Mika, jump at Cas, don't hurt him but jump at him."

Turning, she saw Midnight standing on the floor as a flying monkey and he was jumping. He was all black along with his outfit. He stopped jumping and sat scratching his underarm and then his crotch. He had a wicked grin on his face.

"What did I ever do to you? Don't you want me to be happy?"

Midnight was getting ready to try his vocal cords. He figured a good old chimpanzee screech ought to get that firefighter's attention.

* * * *

Aunt Ernestine was in downtown Boston on the T when she got the cry for help. She wasn't anywhere near her crystal and she was baffled at how she was going to take care of Emma's immediate need.

"Darling, I am nowhere near my crystal… what do you need?"

* * * *

Emma dove at Midnight but he was too quick, he flew onto the counter.

"Why couldn't you be a crow or something harmless, how am I supposed to explain this?"

Midnight could see the firefighter was trying to fight off Mika, who looked like she was doing her best to hump him. *"What a silly cat, if you want to hump him, you do it like this!"* He flew from the counter and landed on Cas.

* * * *

Emma saw the last move and she knew if she couldn't fix this it was probably the end of her relationship with Cas. She sent her arm flying and hoped she could change him back.

As Midnight landed on Cas, he looked down and saw his paws looked like his own paws again of a cat. He went to change himself back to the flying monkey but couldn't. He yowled in protest and with that gave not only Mika a good swipe of his claws, but sunk his claws into Emma's fire fighter's body.

* * * *

"What the hell?" Cas tried to untangle himself from Mika, who seemed to be a bit too amorous for his liking and then he felt the claws of the other cat. Then the two cats were having a fight on his body, which was pinned up against the counter. Where the hell was Emma?

* * * *

Emma took in the situation. She had taken Midnight's powers away for the time being. She ran to Cas, snatched up one fighting cat by the scruff of their neck, saw it was Midnight. Put him down on the floor and sent a silent message to him. *"Go to the other room, NOW!"*

Then she grabbed Mika, who was screeching at the top of her lungs. Nothing like a cat fight and to have it up close and personal in the ears and on one's body. As she grabbed Mika by her scruff and put her down, Mika continued to claw, spit, hiss and screech. *"Go to the living room and sit at the opposite end of the room from Midnight."*

Mika shook herself. "I was only trying to help."

Emma looked down at her other cat. "I know but I have to do damage control."

Emma turned and looked at Cas. His hair, which always looked so wonderfully wavy, looked like he had stuck his finger in a socket, and his shirt was all wet from who knows what and his arms were bleeding and his eyes looked a bit shocked and bugged out.

"I am so sorry! I don't know what came over those two?"

Cas was heading to the sink to wash his arm when he felt Emma's arms around him. He felt her face against his back and he felt her shaking. "I will be okay. Just get me some iodine or something to put on these scratches. They hurt like a bitch right now."

Emma didn't know whether to laugh or cry and she felt like both at this very moment. She reached for the tea tree oil and walked back up to Cas.

"Here let me see." She figured if she kept her hands busy she would be okay.

She washed his arms and then applied the tea tree oil to them. She looked up into Cas's face and saw he had one scratch on his face too. She stood on her tiptoes and kissed it. Then she got the clean paper towel and got it wet with water and soap and started to gently wipe it. "I'm so sorry about my cats."

Cas wrapped his arms around Emma. "Well I told you I fell in love with you despite or even with your cats."

Emma took a deep breath. She really needed to tell him, but how?

Cas could tell something was bothering Emma. Pulling back, he studied her then he tucked his finger under her chin and brought her face up so he could see her eyes. "Hey, what's the matter? I'm not mad about the cats... I don't know why they did that. It's almost like they understood what I was saying." He kissed her trembling lips and saw a tear escape her eye. "It's okay, really."

Emma took one more deep breath and figured now or never. "I have something really important to tell you... I'm not sure how I am going to tell you so I guess I will just show you."

She held his hand and turned. "Please watch."

Emma closed her eyes, sent a silent prayer to the Goddess for help and hoped it all turned out well. She opened her eyes and pushed her hand out towards the counter with all her baking pans. "See Cas, I'm not just a baker, but I have powers. I have since I was born. My Mother, grandmother, all the women in my family back to Eliza Brewster and even before her, had powers." She methodically picked up baking pan after baking pan and sent them to the stove and stacked them quietly and neatly down. Then she called out Midnight. Her cat came and sat and watched her as she picked him up and then he was a flying monkey again.

Midnight couldn't believe it, he was flying. Not just jumping but really flying.

Cas stood with Emma's other hand in his but as he watched what was going on he pulled his hand from hers. He didn't know what to think, he didn't believe in things like this. Sure there was that old show about a witch but this was in front of him and he was now watching her cat fly around the room as a flying monkey.

"So I did see a flying monkey the other morning?"

Emma nodded her head. "Yes, apparently Midnight wanted to get me up so I could feed him and Mika and thought of a way to open the door to my room. He also can understand everything you are saying, so does Mika. So I told Mika to attack you so you wouldn't see Midnight as a flying monkey."

Emma stood still. She had felt Cas release her hand and she felt alone now. She could feel his confusion roll off him like waves and it didn't feel good. She braced herself.

Cas wasn't sure what to do but now he was totally confused. He had fallen in love with someone else, not a witch with a flying monkey.

"I need to go. This is a lot to digest all of a sudden. I don't believe in witches, they don't exist and I don't know what you just did but that's not who I fell in love with."

Emma felt his confusion and now anger hitting her in stormy waves. She bit her lip. "I'm sorry. I never meant to withhold anything from you but it's not something that ever came up. Like I love to bake, knit and oh I am a witch, not just any witch but a hereditary fire starter witch."

Cas felt like he had been sucker punched. "So you started those fires? I've heard everything now. Do you realize what kind of trouble you would be in if I reported you?"

Emma nodded. "I have no control of that power… it was because I saw you…"

Cas had to get out of Emma's house, away from her and away from the cats.

"I thought I had found the one I wanted to be with forever. Maybe you put a spell on me to make me fall in love… maybe all I felt was nothing but a hoax."

"No!" Emma cried out as Cas walked towards the door. "I never put a spell on you and no spell was put on you. My aunt put one on me so I wouldn't catch you all afire or anything else while I was near. You have to believe me." She sucked in her breath and held it because Cas had stopped midstride as he was walking out the door. She watched as he turned and looked at her. His eyes didn't hold the look she had become accustomed to. They looked empty.

"I don't know what to believe anymore. You are no different than other women. Yes you are, you're a witch."

Cas heard himself laugh as he walked out the door. But he found nothing funny. Nothing was funny at this moment. The woman he had let his heart love was supposedly a witch. He wasn't sure what was real anymore.

He climbed up into his truck and after starting it up, pulled out fast, letting his tires squeal down the street.

Chapter 11

Emma sat and cried her heart out to Kathy. Then they both jumped to the door opening and in walked Paul.

"Boy, you really know how to show a guy a great time."

"Oh shut up Paul. Can't you see her heart is broken? She had just told him about her powers and all hell broke loose."

Paul poured himself a cup of coffee and then went and sat down. He watched Emma dry her tears. Then she grabbed her mug and went to the stove. "You know that's why I never let anyone get near me... well that and they would catch afire."

Kathy made a face at her brother. "You need to take a day and go to your aunt's. Take the train and go down. I will stay with the terrors and you can go down and relax and regroup."

Emma nodded. She turned to Paul. "What did he say?"

Paul took his time sipping his coffee. "He came and asked me if I knew about your powers. I told him it was part of my life as you always practiced in front of Kathy and me." He took another sip of his coffee. "He was pretty upset but I told him you didn't deliberately withhold that information. Hell, I told him you were really in love with him and that you would never put a spell on anyone to fall in love with you."

Emma stared at her tea. "What did he say to that?"

Paul shook his head. "He didn't say much but did go in to talk to the Chief about possibly getting done and being transferred out west."

"West?" Both Emma and Kathy said at the same time.

"I knew I should never let my heart fall for him. It was better to bake and have my B&Bs to take care of and have no one in my life, rather than have my heart broken and, and…" she started to cry again.

Kathy looked over at her brother and mouthed the words "Thanks a lot, dipshit."

She wrapped her arms around Emma and let her cry some more.

Paul hit his forehead. "Well I forgot to tell you the Chief has offered him a promotion if he stays. Be made Assistant Chief and if he works out within a year become Chief."

Emma wiped her nose with her hand and Kathy smiled at her friend. "See, it will work out."

Emma shook her head. "It doesn't mean he still loves me."

Kathy smiled and took Emma's mug. "No, but you will have a chance to see him and he will come around, don't you worry."

Paul saw his sister and her best friend. They had been friends forever, ever since the two girls were born. "Hey, I don't want to see you unhappy, Emma. I will continue to put in a good word for you."

Emma nodded and wiped at her nose again. "Kathy, if you don't mind, can you stay tonight? I'm gonna go down and stay tonight at Aunt Tiny's place and talk with her. Then come back late tomorrow night because we have Halloween coming up and I have to make sure everything is just right for Trick or Treat."

Kathy smiled. "Well since you have hired me as your assistant I am gonna prove I can do everything right. Go and come back Halloween morning, give yourself a couple nights down there and it will give you a chance to clear your head. Let Paul and the Chief take care of Cas. Don't worry, everything will work out okay."

Emma hugged her best friend and then Paul. "Thanks you two. I already feel a bit better after talking with you two. Regardless of what happens, I won't try to dwell on it. It is what it is and I can't change his mind. If he doesn't want to be involved with a witch well that means he isn't the one."

Kathy gave her best friend another hug. "Go pack and we will clean up down here."

Emma smiled for the first time in a couple hours. "Okay, I will go pack." She ran out of the kitchen and down the hall.

Kathy looked at her brother. "So what did he say?"

Paul looked at his one and only sister. They shared

just about everything. The more she looked at him the more he felt uncomfortable. "I told you everything."

Kathy gathered up the plates. "No you didn't, I can feel it."

Paul stood. "So have you become a psychic?"

"No, but I know you aren't spilling all of the beans."

Paul came up to his sister and gave her a hug. She pushed him away. "Spill it."

Paul stood for a second and listened. "She can't hear us, can she?"

Kathy shook her head. "No..."

She wasn't entirely sure.

"He was furious with Chief for withholding the information that he knew about Emma and really got upset when he found out Chief knew that she was the one who started the little fires every time she saw him."

Paul poured more coffee. "He said the Chief was as bad as she was for hiding that information."

Kathy shook her head. "Well it's gonna take a miracle to get those two back together."

Paul nodded his head. "But we are up to the challenge."

* * * *

She stood in her front room watching as the little orange car pulled out of the witch's driveway. She watched as it pulled away, and then watched the witch's friend Kathy walk back into the house. Well she knew for certain that witch would be back in plenty of time for Halloween. Now to get the costume ready for her own trick or treating and get everything set. This year would be the last for that witch. She for one would make sure this was a Halloween no one forgot.

* * * *

Aunt Ernestine gave her niece a hug on the door stoop. "Honey, what has you down here on the eve of our best holiday?"

Emma walked in and dropped her small suitcase. "I came because I needed to get out of town for a bit and let my head clear. Kathy is watching the house. Cas and I have broken up and I…" She dissolved into tears.

Ernestine had gotten a warning call from Kathy. She had tried getting in touch with Emma but she had turned off every means of communication. "You know you need to communicate with me. I have tried and tried getting in touch with you but you wouldn't talk or listen."

Emma walked into the kitchen and picked up her aunt's Coon cat. She buried her face in Effie's fur and let the tears flow. "I couldn't…"

Ernestine shrugged her shoulders. "Well if you

don't want to listen to what I have to tell you then don't blame me. You must enjoy hairballs better."

Emma put Effie down and looked up at her aunt. "What do you have to tell me?"

"No, no, no. I will show you. Didn't I tell you trust me? Didn't I tell you everything would be fine and that... Well let me show you. Get yourself a cup of tea and we will go into the parlor."

They sat with the crystal in front of them. "Peek in and see what is in store for you, my beloved niece. You have been a fiery little thing ever since you were born but you have been my only niece and with that comes a special place in our family. You have been given a gift. Do you know after that first night with Cas, I took the spell off and you haven't set anything on fire... well except for his heart."

"Then it was a spell that caught his heart!"

"No Emma, you aren't seeing clearly."

Emma looked into her aunt's crystal. She had never been as good as her aunt when it came to seeing the future. She saw bits and pieces and then she saw something. It couldn't be the present, it certainly wasn't the past... She looked up at her aunt. "I see..."

Her Aunt smiled. "See, I said have faith. Sometimes these things in life take time. Water doesn't come to a boil in an instant... well unless it's us boiling the water. You see, he has been dealt a shock and being a human of the mortal realm he has never had to deal with a woman like you, Emma. He will come around but it's going to take something extraordinary to make him realize he can't live without you. He also has something that he doesn't realize is part of his fiber and very being…" She saw the quizzical look that crossed Emma's face. "You see, I have checked out the man who my niece has fallen in love with. His family moved up from New Orleans. There were two big fires there at the infancy of that beautiful city. His family had come from Ireland. The first O'Halloran who came here to these shores was a pirate. The woman he fell in love with was from the island of Haiti. She was not much darker than him. She was a beautiful woman from all accounts and she was a Voodoo Priestess. When they came together it was said a huge fire would erupt in front of her home. Once it was too much and it burned the French Quarter down. It is also said when he took her as his wife his piracy went well. He had no equal. He finally handed his ship over to his young captain and he retired to a plantation out in the Bayou. When his wife Marie died, he said all desire to stay in Louisiana went with his beloved wife so he told his daughter who was named for her mother that they should move. She was pregnant with her first child but didn't know who the father was."

Emma had pulled her knees up and was sitting on the edge of her seat listening to this story. "So what happened?"

Ernestine was glad she had gotten Emma's mind

off Cas, if for a bit. "They traveled by one of her father's ships to Boston and settled there. Her father became even wealthier in trading, since he had ships of his own. He got the goods for free from what was looted and money from his sugar cane plantation. She had her baby, a baby boy and like our family, where we have only baby girls, little boys were only born in the O'Halloran family."

Emma took her mug and went to the kitchen to make more tea. Effie the Coon cat followed her out. As she measured her tea into the tea ball she saw her aunt come to the kitchen and flick her hand at the kettle. The water came to a boil.

""I don't mind waiting for the water to come to a boil, Aunt Tiny."

Her aunt got some scones that she had made earlier. She got out the jam and cream. "I know you don't mind waiting but we have planning to do and you have to get back home tomorrow."

Emma poured out the water. "So you are kicking your one and only niece out. This is a low day in the Brewster family," she said with a laugh.

Ernestine came up and hugged her niece. "No, I'm not kicking you out, but you need to be back there because I have a feeling these next couple days are going to be pivotal in this relationship. So tomorrow you go home and after this all settles down you can bring him down for a weekend or something."

Emma sipped from her mug and then went to the

table. Effie jumped up on the window seat and meowed at Emma. Emma poured out a bit of tea on a saucer and gave it to the cat. Then she reached for one of the scones her aunt gave her. "So tell me about the powers in Cas's family."

"They can control a certain element too and I have a feeling he is a fire starter also, like yourself. Has he ever said he felt like he was on fire or electrified when you two kissed?"

Emma sat chewing her scone. She felt a smile spread on her face.

Ernestine clapped her hands like an excited child. "I knew it. He and you are meant for one another. You see he can also put the fires out… he was at a fire scene that was in Roxbury." She ran to her laptop at her small table desk and pulled up a newspaper article. "Here it is… Just six months ago. Lt Cas O'Halloran was at the scene of a confirmed structure fire at an apartment complex. He is quoted as saying "I could hear the children screaming and knew they wouldn't be able to get to them in time. One minute there was a wall of fire and then I thought 'how am I going to rescue those children and get my crew out'?" The next instant a crew member said 'the fire started to fizzle out and then it was gone. We all looked at one another and ran for the bedrooms where they heard the screams'. They were able to rescue the children. Then as they walked out of the apartment the place was engulfed again. That wasn't the first time."

Emma sat with a piece of scone in her mouth. She tried to swallow. "Do you think he knows what he is?"

Ernestine shook her head. "I don't know if he even knows his family history. But he is like you but goes a step further. He can stop fires as well as start them. He may just be denying the power because he is afraid."

Emma sat back and felt Effie touching her face with her extra furry paws. Emma leaned into the cat.

"Well I for one am not going to say a thing if I am lucky enough to see him again. It will have to be him bringing it up."

She reached and pulled Effie down onto her lap. The cat never allowed anyone to pick her up but Emma. "You know it's refreshing to see a cat who isn't a familiar… if you knew what I went through with mine…"

Her aunt laughed and came and sat with her. "Honey you were given those familiars for a reason. They have been with your family for a long time. They watch out for you. It may come down to them and you in a situation and it may be life or death. Be thankful for them. I know Midnight is a trial at times but he really has your best interest at heart. He loves you, and Mika will be a powerful familiar someday… if Midnight allows her." Emma smiled and cuddled Effie who sat, eyes closed, enjoying her lap time.

"Kathy was right to send me down here, Aunt Tiny." Emma smiled at her aunt.

Ernestine reached for her niece's hand and gave it a squeeze. "If nothing else, take what you saw in the crystal and have hope everything will be fine. It may be a mess and it may not get better right away but know you and he are destined for each other."

Chapter 12

Emma drove up Route One and made the left onto Route Ninety to make the trip to Cadwell Harbor quicker. She was only a little over 11 miles away now. The sky was a bright blue and she was feeling pretty good. She had the Pointer Sisters playing, she loved their peppy music. She had called Kathy and Kathy had let her know everything was ready for a great Halloween tomorrow. All the candy was bagged up. Kathy had even made the dozens and dozens of cookies and cupcakes for the kids whose parents came in for the little party during Trick or Treat. Emma would get home and get herself prepared for one of the biggest holidays for her and her family. She loved Halloween. She loved the season as the weather got cooler, leaves dropped from the trees. The air had a crisp, clean scent. Kids with their rosy cheeks always stopped by after school to see if she had any *mistakes,* as she called them. It became a habit to make a whole cookie sheet of mistakes for the neighborhood kids. She also let the kids climb and pick apples to snack on. They would pick bushels for her so she would have them for her baking. More times than not the area parents knew where to find their youngsters and would come to Emma to pick up their kids. It was something her mother and Kathy's Mom did back when they were young and she had just carried on the tradition.

She pulled into her driveway and saw her cats sitting in the big window seat. She got out, waved at them. Midnight turned and jumped down. *Hmm, still mad at me...*

As Emma turned she noticed the sheer curtains of Miss Crabtree's house close. *So she has been watching and waiting... Old bat!*

She carried her suitcase in through the carriage house and opened the kitchen door. She smelled baking. She just about fell down when she saw the condition of her kitchen. Kathy turned and she looked like she had been attacked by a bag of flour. She started laughing and then saw Kathy's look.

"Ok, I'm sorry, but you do look pretty funny. What, did the flour attack you or did you jump in?"

Kathy took a dishtowel and wiped at her face. She knew it was a futile attempt to clean herself up. "What, haven't you ever seen someone with a bit of flour on them?"

Emma walked up to her friend and gave her a hug. "It's not a bit of flour I find funny."

She let her arm sweep the room and things started to pick themselves up. "Honey, you are fine. I really appreciate what you have done for me. Take five and we will have a cup of coffee and a treat from Aunt Tiny."

Kathy smiled. "Did she send her sticky buns?"

Emma knew she had Kathy's attention. "Yes. You

know it's the only thing I can't bake like her. She adds something that I can't figure out." She put the pan of sticky buns on the counter and then went and grabbed down two clean mugs.

"So how were the cats?"

Kathy went and grabbed a paper towel to wipe her hands. "Midnight is still pissed at you... I don't know why, well, except for the fact he was changed back to a cat and can't fly. Are you going to give him back his powers?"

Emma shook her head. "No, not yet. I am gonna wait for a few days. Let him learn with powers come a responsibility. He can't just change into a flying monkey because he wants to get me into trouble or to expose my powers. No, I'm gonna let him stew for a day or two at least."

Mika came walking up towards Emma and wrapped herself around Emma's leg. Emma bent and patted her young familiar. *"How goes the battle with him?"*

Mika looked up at Emma. *"He won't talk to me."*

Emma picked up her Torti and hugged her. "Don't take it to heart, he will come around. I am not going to give him his powers back, just yet."

Mika rubbed her face against Emma's and then wiggled to get down.

Emma washed her hands and then sat down to the coffee Kathy had poured. They each cut a sticky bun and placed it on their plates. Emma took the first bite, then Kathy took a bite. They both smiled with a satisfied look as they chewed their bites of sticky buns.

"It's sinful the way those sticky buns taste. She needs to share her recipe so we can create it. I mean, look at all the money that woman from down the coast makes on whoopie pies... Those are really the best whoopie pies in the whole US, maybe even in the whole world."

Emma smiled. I think Aunt Tiny wants her one claim to fame. Everyone down in the Back Bay knows she makes the best sticky buns and whatever she does with them, it's her signature."

Emma sat back and let herself relax. "It's good to be home!"

Kathy smiled at her best friend. "Well I am glad you are back. I really don't know how you do all the baking and have it all taste so good. I mean, I follow your recipe and mine taste fine but it's not your baking. Besides I missed working in the kitchen with you. It's always better having you around."

Emma smiled and finished her bun. "Like I said it's good to be home."

* * * *

Paul was doing truck checks when Cas walked up to him. "Hey, do you want to go get a sandwich? We can walk over to the restaurant and get lunch."

Paul checked off the last item. "Sure. I have one more truck that I can do after lunch."

Cas nodded his head. "I will do the SCBA tanks in the trucks while you are doing that."

Paul climbed out of the main attack engine. "Let's go get lunch."

They sat back after the waitress left with their orders. Paul looked over at his Lieutenant. He didn't know how Cas was in feeling about Emma. He saw him a bit more relaxed but he knew those two needed to be back together. Emma was back at her house and Cas was here. For two weeks they had been inseparable, now they walked as if they were a universe away. Something had to bring them back together, he just wasn't sure what.

"So tomorrow night we will be stationed up on the top of Magnolia Street giving out hats and candy. EMS will be there with us too."

Cas took a sip of his coffee and took the plate the waitress handed him. "It's gonna be different for sure. Being down in the city, we never had a Halloween like Cadwell Harbor has. So where do all the police come from that watch over Emma's and Miss Crabbtree's house?"

Paul sat back after finishing off his sandwich. "They have a signup go around the different departments and the Sherriff's department sends some too. One of the State Troopers lives at the other end of Magnolia so he is on duty that night. He has four young children and he has a little party there too for all their friends from school."

Cas nodded. "I can only imagine what it's gonna be like." He thought about how excited Emma had been getting with Halloween coming up. He missed her and her smile. He missed her sleeping next to him. He missed their spooning and how they would wake up in the middle of the night and make love. He missed her.

Paul could see Cas was thinking and if he was a betting man he would bet he was thinking about Emma.

"I will be right back," Cas said. He got up to go to the rest room.

Paul sat for a second and then he had a thought. He sent a text to Emma's Aunt Tiny and then sat back with a smile.

Cas got back and sat down and then drank down the rest of his coffee. Then he signaled the waitress for their check just as the tones went off.

"Cadwell Harbor Fire, Cadwell EMS, CO_2 alarm at 66 Magnolia."

Paul wiped his face took out some money threw it down on the table. Cas did the same. They ran out and ran to the Utility truck that was parked out front.

"Cadwell Utility One to Cadwell Dispatch, en-route to 66 Magnolia."

"Cadwell Dispatch… copy that."

"Cadwell Engine One en-route to 66 Magnolia."

"Cadwell Dispatch... copy that"

Cas drove up to the top of Main Street and pulled a U-turn and then they took a right onto Mechanic Street. They turned onto Free Street and then Magnolia and were at the driveway in a couple seconds.

"Cadwell Utility One on Scene. Two story, wood frame construction, single family dwelling. Will be off investigating. Car 3 has command."

"Paul get the meter and bring a P-can just in case."

Cas was just about to knock at the door when he was met at the door by Paul's sister Kathy.

"I'm sorry I have been having a time of it with Emma's oven. She won't come out. She says she has to figure out the problem so she can continue to bake..."

Cas looked in, saw the smoke and saw the burnt offering that was smoking from the oven. "I will handle it."

He walked in, walked to the window and flung it open and then turned on the fan above the stove. "Here let me take that." he put on one of his gloves and then took the pan, brought it outside the door and threw it on the grass. He walked back in and saw Emma with her head in the oven. He looked at Paul. "Take readings..."

He picked up Emma and brought her kicking and screaming outside. "Have you lost your marbles? You could become overcome with carbon monoxide." He placed her down and held onto her as she tried to go back into her house. "Emma, listen to me!" He held her there till she looked up at him. "You need to stay outside till we can figure out why the CO_2 alarm went off." He could see she was mad but he was just doing his job.

Turning to one of the EMS staff. "Check out Emma here to make sure she is okay." Seeing Emma's face and that of the EMT he added. "Don't release her till I give the okay."

He could see Emma was struggling with his order. "Do as I say. Your house is my house till I give the okay. So go get checked out... now!"

He turned to go back in the house.

Emma stuck her tongue out at him and then turned back to the EMT. "I'm fine, really I am..."

Mark Smith, who was new to the area, took one look at the disheveled redhead in front of him and could see she was a handful. "Well let's just make sure you are fine. Until the lieutenant releases your home, you are to stay with me."

Emma grunted. "He's doing that because he is mad at me..."

Mark started writing down information on his clipboard. "Well until he gives me the clear, you are my guest in my ambulance."

Kathy stood in the doorway because her brother and Cas wouldn't let her back in. They were checking the kitchen with their meter but not finding anything wrong.

Paul scratched his head. "I don't get it, the meter showed there was a presence of a probable gas leak, now it doesn't show anything."

"Get the spray bottle of dish soap and let's go around and check her fittings. It will show us if there is a leak."

* * * *

She ran from the front to the back of her house and found what she was looking for. She loosened the fitting and then went back in her house. Those nosy firemen would figure the problem was coming from her house and would tell her to get out... then she wouldn't be watched. She would be free to finish off that witch. Everyone thought she was a helpless old woman. "I may be old but I'm not old and senile like they think."

She packed up some things and then put the suitcase in her closet. It would be just a matter of time.

* * * *

Cas stood outside by Utility One. "Well, I just don't get it. Your meter showed a reading. Where were you when you got the reading?"

Paul turned. "I was inside the door. I hadn't turned

it on till I was right near the door so I would get a correct reading."

Cas nodded. "I thought so."

Paul smiled to himself. He would have to text Aunty Tiny and thank her.

Emma was wiping her hands, looking over at Kathy. She saw Kathy, standing looking out the window. She walked over, looking out, she saw Paul and Cas standing out front talking. She sighed. She missed him so much but it wasn't her problem. It was his and he had to come to her.

Kathy stayed there. She was praying the guys would look back. She knew something had to happen to get Cas and Emma back together. She stood there and then she saw them both look up and sniff the air. Then she saw Cas say something to Paul and she saw Paul turn on the meter he had in his hands. "Emma, something is wrong, look."

Emma watched. "I am sure it's nothing."

Kathy saw them take off in a run across the street to old lady Crabtree's house. "Yes there is something wrong. They have gone to Crabtree's house."

Emma ran to the other window to get a better look and could see Paul holding the meter. He then yelled to Cas. Emma watched as Cas ran up the front steps.

Cas pounded on the front door of Miss Crabtree's house. "Cadwell Harbor Fire Department."

He stood what seemed forever and then he heard a feeble reply.

"I'm coming," Miss Crabtree smiled before opening the door.

"What can I do for you? Oh, it's *you!* You are the one I always see over at the witch's house."

Cas could feel the hate the woman had for Emma. He was just doing his job but he didn't like the feeling he got from this old lady. If he were a meter he would be off the screen with the hate she was emitting from her soul.

"Miss Crabtree, we are getting high readings of a propane leak here. We think your leak is the cause of Miss Brewster's alarms going off." He knew it wasn't but it seemed to be strange that the two would have problems the same day. He had to find out.

"So if you don't mind we are going to check your house. I am also having EMS check you out."

He watched as Miss Crabtree tottered down the stairs, the EMS attendant took her hand and he saw her smile up at him. It looked evil. He shook himself.

"Hey Lieutenant, We have readings that are off the charts in her house. She can't go back in for at least 24 hours so to make sure it's aired out."

Cas went to the truck and packed up with his air pack. Then, putting his SCBA mask on, tightening it down, he attached it to his regulator. **"Ok let's go find the leak."**

They were down in the basement where they found

the worst readings. They checked all the fittings and then found what they were looking for.

"Bingo!"

Cas gave Paul the thumbs up sign.

They got to the kitchen and saw the Chief packing up. **"Hold up Chief,"** Cas said over the radio.

Cas, followed by Paul, got out of the house and pulled the Chief along with them till they got up to Utility 1. Cas disconnected his respirator. "Chief, we have to keep Miss Crabtree out of that house for at least twenty-four hours to air it out."

The Chief looked at his Lieutenant "Whatever you think. If it will make things work easier. We can keep her out till after Halloween."

Cas nodded after taking off his mask. "Yea, that would work better. The gas company should come and do a thorough check."

The chief smiled a rueful smile. This will be the first year that old Miss Crabtree won't be on Magnolia for the festivities."

Cas pulled his Chief to the side. "I am no specialist, but that woman is walking with hate for Emma. I can feel it."

Chief nodded. "Yes, it's only gotten worse. She is by far the worst Crabtree this town has seen." Chief looked at his Lieutenant. He looked tired. "Why don't you go check on Emma? I am sure she would love to hear her arch nemesis will be off the street."

Cas shook his head. "Why don't you do that,

Chief? I think she has seen enough of me for one day. She was calling me every name in the book for carrying her out of her house."

Chief laughed. "I can only imagine. But it comes with the job. Man up, Cas, if you are in this job you have to take the good with the bad. Emma is only upset because this is one of her busiest times of year for baking."

Cas looked at his chief. "How long have you known about her powers?"

The Chief grabbed the clipboard, heard Miss Crabtree cackle. "That is my definition of a witch." He pointed at Emma's neighbor. I have known about Emma, her mother and her grandmother and their powers as long as I can remember. Her grandmother was the sweetest woman alive and everyone loved her, like they do Emma's mother and Emma herself." He looked at his Lt closely. "You need to make up, you are missing out on a wonderful woman. She has never dated until you. You two are meant for each other."

Cas stood there thinking. "I will go tell her about her neighbor but that's it. I have to get all this magic stuff clear in my head."

Paul came up to Cas and their Chief. "I have 65 Magnolia marked off with caution tape. The gas company will be here later to work on the leaks and check the whole system out. Miss Crabtree is going to the Inn on Main Street to stay till day after tomorrow."

Cas picked up his air tank. "Paul I will be with you in a minute. I'm just going to go over and tell Emma that her neighbor will be gone."

Cas walked over to Emma's house. He would tell her and then go right back to the station.

* * * *

"Emma, Cas is coming up the drive." Kathy looked over at Emma, who was beating the hell out of her bread dough by hand kneading it instead of putting it in the machine. She knew when her friend was upset, she always made bread.

Seeing no reply, "Okay, I will get the door."

She ran to the door and saw Cas just about to knock on it. "Hey Cas."

Cas looked past Kathy. "Can I see Emma or is she too busy?"

Emma looked over at the door. "You are welcome to come in if you don't mind coming into a witch's house."

Cas swore under his breath.

"I can hear that!" Emma said as she wiped her face. She knew there must be flour all over her but she didn't care. It wasn't like she was trying to impress him.

"What can I do for you, Lieutenant O'Halloran?"

Oh, so we are back to that? Cas thought.

"I just wanted to let you know, Miss Brewster, that your neighbor will be gone till the day after tomorrow so maybe you will have a quiet Halloween."

Emma saw Kathy leave the room. Drat, why was she leaving like that when she needed her presence?

"Thanks for letting me know."

Cas really missed Emma, but he couldn't be sure it was a real feeling or a spell she had put on him. He still needed to sort out his feelings. "Well, have a good day." He turned and was almost at the door when he heard.

"I've missed you, Cas."

He stopped, almost turned but knew if he saw her eyes he would be sunk. "Yeah, I've..." He couldn't say it so walked out and closed the door. *Yea, I've missed you too baby but I'm not letting you know that. I don't know what is real.*

Emma stood there. She felt the verbal slap. Well, she was not gonna let that bother her. She threw her hand in the air and a whirlwind of flour started spinning. "He thinks he can just start to say something and not finish what he was going to say."

Kathy came back down and saw Emma in the midst of a whirlwind. She had numerous bowls all getting mixed up. And she was in the middle beating that same bread dough to death.

Kathy walked in between the bowls that were in midair dodging the ones that were spinning like they were on a mixing machine.

She put her hand out and touched Emma's hand. Sparks shot out. Kathy laughed. "It's been a while since I've seen you this mad."

Emma bit her lip. "Yeah, remind me if I am ever stupid enough to fall for someone, that I need my ass kicked."

Kathy held out her arms and Emma collapsed in her arms for a hug. Then she started to cry.

Kathy held her friend and let her cry. She patted her back and said things that friends say to friends when they need it the most.

Emma snuffed up her nose. "I am glad I have you for my best friend."

Kathy laughed. "Yeah, just keep your boogers to yourself."

Emma snorted. "Yea but you didn't say keep your bread dough to yourself." She picked up a hunk of bread dough and smashed it on Kathy's head, working it in.

Kathy looked at her with shock and then she glanced to her side and grabbed a spinning bowl. She took the whisk out of the bowl and snapped it so cake batter went all over Emma's face. Emma stood right there. Then she smiled and licked at the batter. "Mmm, that tastes good but it would taste better if I added some raspberry." She snapped her finger and she had a bowl of mashed raspberries. She poured the bowl over Kathy's head. Kathy shrieked and then began the epic battle of the two best friends having a food fight.

Paul stood ready to get into the Utility truck when he heard a scream from Emma's house and figured it was Kathy. Then he heard Emma's scream. "You are in so much trouble, Kathy." *Emma will be better, food fights between friends always help.*

Cas got into Utility One. "Do you think they are okay? I mean listen to them and Kathy is calling Emma a friggin' witch."

Paul laughed. "You need to know Emma and Kathy. They love one another like sisters. They are just having a food fight."

Cas started the engine. "Food fight? Well I for one would like to see that."

Paul looked over at his Lieutenant "Get back with her then."

Cas shook his head. "It's not that easy. I don't know if I can trust her. She could have put a spell on me."

Paul shook his head. "You've got it all wrong, she would never do that. Her aunt may have put a spell on her to make sure she didn't catch you on fire when she touched you. You see…"

"Hold that thought," Cas said.

"Cadwell Harbor Utility One to Cadwell Harbor Dispatch"

"Cadwell Harbor Dispatch…"

"We are clear of 66 and 65 Magnolia. All Cadwell

Harbor units are back in service."

"Copy that Cadwell Harbor Utility One."

Cas pulled up to the stop sign. Looking over at Paul he knew he was a friend of Emma's but just from the little he had known him he seemed like a good friend, one that he could count on in good and bad. Someone who he could count on to cover his back if he needed it.

"Okay, so tell me Paul what you know and how you are sure Emma never put a spell on me, and what's this about her aunt?"

Paul knew it was going to be a long story. "Are you up for a long story?"

Cas nodded as they pulled up in front of the station. "Yes, tell me while we get everything cleaned up."

"So you see Aunt Tiny…"

Cas laughed. "Aunt Tiny?"

Paul smiled. "Yea, Aunt Ernestine is Aunt Tiny. She lives down in Boston in the Back Bay. It's been the family home in Boston forever. I have spent as much time there as I have at my own relatives. She knows about Emma's strengths and weaknesses. One of those weakness is when she saw a guy that she was really attracted to she would ask her aunt to place a spell on her to make sure she didn't catch things on fire. When you first saw her…"

Cas put the new air tank in auxiliary holding spot for extras and put his pack back on the truck. "I first saw her at the bagel shop. It was pouring out and she was trying to open the door as I was going out. I was kinda rude cause the rain was dripping off the overhang and dripping onto her," he smiled. "She then said 'Excuse me but when you think you are finished ogling me would you mind terribly getting out of my way so I don't melt out here'."

Cas laughed as he made a note on his check list. "I could have sworn I heard a cat his…"

Paul put his water bottle down. "You probably heard Midnight."

"I didn't see him."

Paul shook his head. "No, he probably had made himself invisible, he is her familiar."

Cas walked to his desk at the back of the apparatus bay. Sitting down he got out his Webster dictionary and then clicked on his computer. "Okay, hold on a minute…"

Cas did some typing and said, "Look, it says in the Catholic church that a familiar is a person who renders services in a pope's or bishop's household or a member of a high official's staff. In Emma's instance I guess this would be the definition, a spirit to serve or guard a person." Cas sat back. So are you telling me Midnight guards her?"

Paul smiled. "Yes, he has always been there for her. When she went off to college down in Boston he yowled for days till she came home and brought him with her. One day he brought this half drowned kitten into her house on an early March morning. It was sleeting real bad and you should have seen Emma. She was beside herself. She was determined to save that kitten."

"So is that her second familiar, Mika?"

"Yup, Mika is a familiar in training though Midnight won't give over too much power to her."

Cas buried his head back in his hands. "I just don't know what to believe. I have tried all my life to stay away from this kind of stuff."

Paul leaned forward on his Lieutenant's desk. "What do you mean?"

"He means this…"

Both jumped to the sound of the Chief's voice. "Maybe Cas would like to tell you about this. He is running from a gift or power of his own. Boy, the pot is calling the kettle black."

Cas looked at the headlines. City Fire Fighter, STOPS Fire, rescues children…

Paul quickly scanned the article. "Okay bro, so you have been holding out on us. You need to go talk to her."

Cas looked up at his Chief. "Thanks a lot, Chief."

"I know when I see a couple that needs to be together. I don't profess to understand everything but I have seen enough and been around Emma and her family all my life. They aren't bad and neither are you. You both have extra strengths and gifts, use them."

"Okay, I will go talk to her tomorrow night at Trick or Treat."

Paul shook his head. "Why not now?"

Cas stood up. "No, after work I am going to get some things together for her. I have a lot of explaining to do and since tomorrow night is a Friday I am going to do it in grand style."

Chapter 13

Emma sat and finished reading her ancestor's diary. She was tired. Midnight and Mika were curled up on the foot of her bed. Emma sighed. She got up and put the diary back in her little safe. There was her family's spell book that had been in her family since the original Eliza. Her Aunt Ernestine had given it to her when she had graduated from college. She pulled it out, opened and sniffed the old pages. She sneezed and it blew the pages till it landed on a page in the middle.

Emma read the spell. *"A protection spell?"* She saw Midnight open his eyes. Emma had seen this spell but had never said it. She felt no need for protection. Her life had always been pretty low key and calm. Even with the old bat across the street. She read it in her head.

Storms may come
The winds will blow
Lightning comes from the skies
Fire may surround me
But say these words
Love will save me
Love will save me
Love will save me
And I will be safe

Emma said the spell again, but out loud.

"Storms may come
The winds will blow
Lightning comes from the skies
Fire may surround me
But say these words
Love will save me
Love will save me
Love will save me
And I will be safe."

Emma smiled. She put the book back in the safe and then went and climbed back up on the bed. Snapping her finger, her light went out. She felt Midnight come and curl up around her head. She smiled. "I love you, Midnight."

"I love you too Emma... I am sorry I ruined things for you."

Emma turned so she had her face covered by Midnight. She started to cry. "If only love would save me..."

Midnight closed his eyes. He had to figure a way to help his witch.

* * * *

She crept along the side of the house, furthest from that nosy firefighter Paul. She had been planning this for a year. She knew Emma's habits and that of her cats. They slept with her so she could prowl all she wanted and no one would bother her. She got to the bulkhead and lifted it. She had it well-oiled so it was nice and quiet. She would make sure no one knew she was the one who started this fire. If anything, this house along with the witch and her cats would go up so fast. She had seen the old gas can down in Emma's basement. What a perfect thing to have on hand. There would be no fingerprints because she was wearing gloves. She had to control herself from laughing. This was going to be so easy, she whispered to herself. She crept down and then turned on her head lamp. She put it on the green lamp. She picked up the gas can. "Good, full..."

She started to spread a line. She had a good amount along the outer wall. Being an old house the fire would travel up the walls and that was the wall where Emma's room was located. She already had gas spread all along the outer perimeter of the house. She spread newspapers that had been stored down in the basement. This would add to the whole effect. Putting the gas can down she surveyed her work. "Good riddance."

She walked out. She was about to light a match when she heard thunder. As she struck the match a great bolt of lightning came out of the sky and hit one street over. *Perfect... as long as it doesn't rain till it's too late.*

She struck another match and then as she walked around the house she continued to light matches. Then she got into her car and checked everything. She would be gone and nobody would know where she was. They could point fingers but they had nothing on her. Everything would be destroyed in the fire. She would see it on the news and it gave her immense pleasure. "The place would be a better place without Emma Brewster." She let out a howl of laughter and started up the car. Driving slowly away she could see the glow grow in her rearview mirror. She continued to laugh as she drove up the street.

* * * *

Paul got up to take a leak when he jumped at the reflection in the mirror. The sky was all ablaze. He turned and looking out the window. "Emma!"

He grabbed his phone and called 911.

"Cadwell Harbor Dispatch…"

"Confirmed Structure Fire at 66 Magnolia. This is Paul…"

Paul was running out his door in his shorts. As he ran he screamed Emma's name.

* * * *

Emma was dreaming that it was summer, her least favorite season because it was always so hot. Then she heard a yowling. She tried pulling herself out of the fog but it was hard. She finally opened her eyes because she felt a weight on her chest. Opening her eyes she saw Midnight and the room was lit up with flames. Then she heard thunder. She jumped up. "Midnight what the hell?" She jumped up but she felt heat under her feet. She saw fire climbing outside. She looked around and knew maybe their only hope was get to the attic. "Midnight, where is Mika?"

Midnight hated this. He had been in a few fires with his other witches and it never turned out well. *"I sent her out. Told her to save herself. I will never leave you."*

Emma tried throwing her hands out at the fire but nothing she came up with was working. So she thought of her aunt. She picked up Midnight and ran for the door. As soon as she went across the floor she heard its groans and creeks and flames started to shoot up through the floor along the edge. "Midnight, why didn't my fire alarms go off?"

She touched the door handle with the back of her hand and found it warm but not hot. She opened the door a little. Saw smoke. "Midnight, get on my back, we are going to crawl up the attic stairs."

She got to the attic door and got up. She could feel Midnight's claws in her back as he hung onto her tee shirt. If this was the only pain she felt that would be okay.

They crawled up the stairs and then when she got up to the top saw just a little smoke. "Let's get to the window. It's on the opposite side as my room and hopefully there won't be any flames like on my side of the house."

"I'm gonna kill that old witch when I get my paws on her." Midnight thought.

Emma tried prying the window but it had been shut for so many years it wouldn't give. "Midnight, we need something to break this."

"Use your powers…"

Emma threw her hands out but nothing happened. *"Aunty I NEED HELP!"*

* * * *

Ernestine woke with smoke swirling around her nose. "Now what?" She sat up in bed and the smell of smoke and gasoline were so strong she thought her own home was on fire. She saw Effie, her Coon cat, calmly washing her paws. She saw a small brown lump and looked closer and saw it was a dead mouse. "Thanks Effie, but take your little offering to the basement." She got up, grabbed her wrapper and walked at a brisk pace down the stairs. If she was smelling smoke and gasoline it wasn't good.

She got up to her crystal and saw it glowed. "Oh Goddess, no." She then heard Emma's voice scream through the flames.

"Emma, where are you?"

Emma started to cough. The smoke was getting worse, even up in the attic. She had thrown an old crate against the window but for some reason that wouldn't even break the window. "Aunty, my magic is gone. I can't get anything to work. I can't even break a window in the normal way."

Ernestine didn't like that. *"Where are you?"*

Emma coughed some more. *"I am over by the hole that leads into the crawl space over the carriage house. If Midnight and I can get through there, we will be safe or…"*

"Hold on Emma, help is on the way."

She stared at her crystal that almost leaped off the table with the flames that were getting bigger as she watched. She started to chant an old spell to bring rain.

She watched the clouds that were already building up in the west pull together. Thunder boomed and lightning streaked across the sky. Then she saw Miss Crabtree. She was in her car. She sent a lighting bolt towards her car and a moose was there on the side of the road. "I am sorry moose, but I need to sacrifice you for the greater good. We need to stop that woman. She needs to spend time behind bars, not in a retirement home."

* * * *

Cas pulled up with a screech of his tires and jumped out. He started pulling on his gear and as he did that, tried scanning the growing crowd. He didn't see any redheads anywhere present. He pulled out his mask and as he ran, he got up to the Chief, who was already barking orders. Mutual aid companies were pulling up, setting up their lines and coming to report to Cadwell Harbor's Chief.

"Chief, have you seen Emma?"

Chief looked over at him. "No, Paul is gearing up too. You two are going to need to do a preliminary search. Bring in an uncharged line and find that girl and for god sakes you get her and you two out alive."

Paul had his air tank on, his SCBA mask on tight as it would go. He hooked his respirator to his mask and took a breath., air was flowing. He had his helmet on when he saw Cas come up with an uncharged hose. Each of them grabbed a tool and headed for the side door that led to the kitchen.

Cas had seen the ladder truck making a set to the second story window, which would be Emma's room. One of the mutual aid departments had another uncharged line and would go in behind them in a counter-clockwise preliminary search pattern. He saw a RIT team all set for both crews that were going in.

"Crew O'Halloran going in to do a preliminary search clockways .We will do sides A and B."

"Copy that. Get her and get out."

"Copy."

Cas tapped Paul. They both brought their heads together and, tapping each other on their masks, started in.

"We will go as far as we can walking, then get down on our knees."

Paul gave Cas the thumbs up. They moved through the kitchen and Cas directed the other crew to go to the dining room to the right. **"Do sides C and D."**

"Copy that Lieutenant."

Cas could see the whole living room ablaze. *If Emma was in there she didn't survive.*

"Crew Smith, knock that down…"

They turned and went to the staircase. Taking his ax, Cas sounded each and every step as they went upstairs. Even though it was only smoky, with the fire to the back of the wall in the living room it could have weakened things and then he saw fire shooting up through the tread just in front of them.

"Damn, move it now!"

They took the last three stairs in a giant step and stood on the upper landing. Emma's room was ahead of them. Cas got down on his knees and sounded the floor, knowing the seat of the fire was below them. The floor still seemed sturdy. They got halfway in and the floor started to feel spongy. Cas turned and looked at Paul. He held up his finger.

He got up and with his head lamp saw her bed. He gave the blankets a vicious yank. Nothing came with it but blankets.

"Crew O'Halloran. We are on the second floor but still no sign of her. Going for the attic."

* * * *

Kathy jumped out of her car and went running up barefoot to the Chief. She tapped him on the shoulder. "Chief, where is Emma?"

Cadwell Harbor's Chief looked over at Emma's best friend. He had watched the two of them grow up. "We don't know, they haven't found her, so please don't panic."

"Don't panic? That's my best friend's house and you tell me not to panic and she is in there somewhere!"

She started to scream Emma's name.

Emma was trying to pull up the floor boards because she knew if they could get down into the carriage house or barn it would be okay. The floor felt cool. Thankfully the old bitch hadn't for some reason set this part of the house afire. She coughed and looked over at Midnight. *"Save yourself. You can get through that hole over there."*

"No, I am yours for life. We will get out alive or go to the other side together."

Emma placed a kiss on her Midnight's head. *"There has got to be something here to tear up this floor board."* Emma laid her head down and could just make out the flashing lights coming up through the crack and she could feel the cool breeze coming up through the cracks. She crawled back and closed the door to this part of the attic. That would slow things down a bit and maybe Paul would know to search for her here.

The Chief was standing, directing one of his crews to make a trench cut to cut off the carriage house and barn from the main part of the house when Kathy tapped him on the shoulder. "Have them cut into the roof at the carriage house. There is a crawl space that Emma and I used to go into to hide from Paul. Paul knows about it too. Tell them to get to there, that's where Emma is, I can almost feel it."

The Chief looked at Kathy's face. She was crying and her face was smudged with soot that was blowing with the wind that had started up with the storm that was quickly brewing up from the west.

"Incident Command to Crew O"Halloran."

"Crew O'Halloran to IC."

"Get to the crawlspace between the attic and the carriage house. Kathy said that's where Emma is. She said Paul will know."

"Copy that IC."

* * * *

Paul went ahead of Cas and crawled quickly. He had visions of when he and the girls would play hide and seek. The girls when they were really little would always go there.

"This way."

Paul crawled and got up to the door, reaching up he pulled on the handle of the door. It gave way and they peeked in.

* * * *

Emma lay down. She never thought it would be like this. Her hands were bleeding she was sure from trying to pull the boards apart. She didn't care. She and Midnight, who she had tucked under her, were laying there. She wasn't going out of this world alone. Maybe in the next life she would meet up with that old bat and get back at her for killing her and her beloved familiar. She hoped Mika had gotten out safely.

She started to feel sleepy. The smoke had done something to her brain because even their hideaway was filling up with smoke. And she couldn't think clearly. All she wanted to do was sleep.

As she started to fall asleep she could hear thunder and then pounding and then she thought she heard Mika but that would be silly because she had escaped.

* * * *

Mika crawled through the little hole and saw the body of her Emma. She ran up to her.

"Wake up, Help is coming... Wake up Emma! Wake up! Midnight, wake up!"

Cas and Paul crawled into the little crawl space. It wasn't high enough for them to stand, only children could.

"Crew O'Halloran to Incident Command, We found her. Get some back up over the carriage house."

"Copy that Crew *O'Halloran*!"

The Chief looked at Kathy. "See I told you they would find her."

"Is she okay?"

Chief hoped she was.

Cas picked up Emma and found she was limp. Her cat was under her. He moved a bit and he saw Midnight open his eyes.

"Paul, let's get us out of here."

Paul saw Mika and knew she probably knew of the really small hole that went to the barn.

"Cas tell Chief to get someone in the barn, have them make a hole just at the hay loft connecting to the carriage house."

Paul started using his halligan to pry the floor boards up.

He turned to the sound of the fire that was eating up the door behind them.

Cas held Emma's limp body. He had felt a pulse but it wasn't strong. He pushed the button on the radio.

"Crew O'Halloran here, need a RIT crew in

the barn up in the hay loft, break a hole that connects the barn to the carriage house. We have Emma and her cats but Emma is unconscious. We need EMS."

"Copy that!"

The Chief looked at Kathy. "You stay put. We will get them out."

Kathy watched as the Chief went running off to get the RIT crew going.

For a brief second all the noise stopped as another radio transmission came over the radio.

"MAYDAY, MAYDAY, MAYDAY. We are out of air and trapped!"

The Chief got back on the radio. "Copy. All Engines signal for the mayday and evacuation of Crew Smith. RIT CREW, get in the barn loft, break a hole that connects the carriage house."

Kathy stood there and then jumped to all the engines signaling a **MAYDAY.**

All of the engines up and down the street blew their horns three sharp, short tones.

Then as if on cue, the heavens opened up and with a flash of lightning a deluge started.

* * * *

Ernestine packed her Audi and with a quick look at her gas knew she was going to be up in Maine in record time. She looked at Effie who was in her crate.

She would drop her off at her friend Violet's house and then she was off. She waved her hand over her crystal and saw the lighting and the rain. She flicked her hands at the crystal again and could hear the thunder and the downpour in Cadwell Harbor.

* * * *

Cas had Emma's body in his arms. Paul had made a hole in the floor and a firefighter poked his head up through.

"We have a ladder, pass her down."

Cas knew by looking at his respirator monitor that he was almost out of air because his vibe alert had gone off. But he was going to get everyone out.

"Make the hole bigger. I'm bringing her down, I'm not letting her go." He watched as one of the guys gave a chain saw to Paul who cut the hole wider.

"Ok, let's get out of here."

Cas directed Paul and the cats. The cats needed no prompting. He saw Midnight look back once and knowing Cas had Emma, he jumped down the hole. He was down on the ladder with Emma over his shoulder.

Emma was feeling funny. She felt like she was going to throw up. She was on someone's shoulder with her head hanging upside down. She heard what sounded like Darth Vader and then she saw one of her cats land on the barn floor. Blissfully cool air blew in and she heard thunder and saw a streak of lightning. She felt herself being brought off the person's shoulder and then she was placed on a stretcher and she was moving though rain. She stretched her face to let the rain hit her and she opened her eyes. There over her was Cas. He had on a mask, but she knew it was him. Next as they lifted her up into the ambulance he climbed up to her side.

Cas had to get the mask off, had to kiss her face, even if she didn't want a kiss, he was going to kiss her and if he was lucky enough, kiss her every day for the rest of his life.

"I am so sorry Emma. I was an ass but if you will give me another chance I will be by your side for the rest of your days." He saw her eyes and they started to smile.

"Lieutenant, we need to work on her. If you could just sit there, you can have her after we determine her condition."

Emma reached for his hand as he sat down. He let the crew work on her.

Kathy ran up to the back of the ambulance. She looked in and saw Cas holding Emma's hand. She climbed up in. "Emma!"

Chapter 14

Cas held Emma close. He hadn't let go of her once since the EMS crew had cleared her. She refused transport so there wasn't much they could do for her. She said she would be in good hands with Lieutenant O'Halloran.

"I'm never going to let you go."

Emma laughed. "Well you might have to if you want to go to the bathroom or to work."

Cas kissed Emma's pert little nose. "You know what I mean. I am so sorry and I have so much to tell you." He saw her eyes twinkling and felt her little hands working in his turnout coat. "But I have something to ask you."

Emma smiled. She buried her face on his chest and sniffed at his shirt. "I've missed you."

Cas nodded. "I know and I don't want to ever fight with you again."

Emma smiled. "We will but not like that. Now ask me what you wanted to ask me."

Cas felt the rain start to get heavy again. "We need to get you under cover."

Emma shook her head. "No, I want to be out here in the rain. Do you know how good it feels? Now ask me." She smiled and kissed Cas's lips, letting her lips linger on those wonderful lips that while she was slipping away from life, she felt them tug to bring her back to life.

Cas smiled down at Emma. She was getting soaked but as the rain poured down on them he took a deep breath. 'Will you marry me, Emma Brewster? I know it's quick but I know one thing. I can't live without you."

Emma smiled and nodded her head and leaned into him "Yes!"

They stood as the rain poured down over them.

"Love saved me."

Cas smiled, "Yes and it saved me too."

He kissed her, taking her lips like it was his life line. It was. He needed her as much as the air he breathed.

"I love you, Emma Brewster!"

Emma looked up, rain was pouring down, she had all she could do to see but she smiled up to Cas. She let her hands take his face as she kissed him soundly and felt the bolt that was zinging back and forth through the two of them, then hitting her heart. She was in love and gone. Like a star bursting forth in the sky and sharing its light. She was going to be spending a lifetime sharing her love and heart.

"I love you, Cas O'Halloran.

The End

Epilogue

Emma felt Cas wrap his arms around her as she placed the Christmas turkey on the table. The sun shone bright on the lake that their house was on.

"Have I told you how much I love you, Emma Brewster-O'Halloran?"

Emma smiled. "Yup, you told me first thing when you crawled on top of me this morning. I told you I want those wake ups every morning."

Cas smiled and rubbed her tummy. "Well once you get bigger I won't be crawling on top of you."

Emma turned in his arms. "I don't care, as long as you wake me up kissing me and loving me."

Kathy came walking into the dining room. "Hey you two, Chief and his wife are here. He says he has a present for you both."

Emma looked up at Cas. "What do you suppose it is?"

Cas smiled. "I don't know, maybe if we go into the living room we will find out." He took her hand and led her.

Emma yelled over her shoulder, "Auntie, come with us to the living room."

Emma and Cas went and sat on the sofa. Aunt Ernestine came and sat next to them. The Chief, his wife, along with Paul and Kathy and their dates sat on the other couch.

The Chief reached over to Emma and gave her a flat package, wrapped in shiny red wrapping. "I was hoping to get this. Even though we knew it was going to be this outcome it settles things nicely." He gave the package to Emma and watched as she and Cas opened it.

Emma read the report. She gave it to Cas who scanned the pages. "We knew, but it's nice to know they determined the cause arson. So that means that old witch is locked away for the rest of her life?"

The Chief nodded. "Yes, she was lucky she didn't get killed by that moose. She is only seventy-two so she could live another twenty years."

Emma nodded her head. "In a way I feel bad for her. Something must have made her get really twisted."

Chief cleared his throat. "She said in the closed hearing that once she got jilted by your grandfather she was on a lifelong quest to destroy your family. She faked being senile so no one would suspect her. The police found files on her laptop that she kept hidden that she had researched how to pull off the fire."

Emma shivered. "I can't even imagine her brain or anyone's brain working like that. I don't understand hate and how some people can be so hate filled and just want to hurt people. People really have a bad conception of witches and how they use their powers. Yes, there are bad in every walk in life but it's hard for me to wrap myself around it."

Emma was pulled in for a hug from Cas.

Cas kissed Emma's temple. Then he got up to add more wood to the fire.

"You know, that fire showed me that you were the most important part of me and you really completed me. I've been running from my powers all my life, afraid that I would be different. I was little when I found out about those powers. I was so afraid of the mean kids in school who talked about all the different kids and teased them. I just buried them, hoping if I ignored them long enough they would go away." He looked over at his wife. "You made me whole, Emma."

Emma blew a kiss to Cas.

Ernestine smiled at her growing family. Emma's parents were due in later. They didn't know Emma was expecting. She smiled and rubbed Emma's little belly. She was glad to see she had stopped wearing her corsets. She just wore her peasant blouses. "I'm so happy for you both, honey."

Emma reached over and hugged her aunt. "Thank goodness I have an open line to you Auntie. You helped save me as much as everyone else."

Ernestine shook her head. "No honey, it was all Cas and Paul. I just brought the rain."

Paul stood up with his glass of wine. 'Well I propose a toast to our new family in our midst." He motioned for Cas to go back with Emma.

Emma wrapped her arm around Cas.

Paul smiled. "To my Lieutenant who is one great firefighter. I never felt like we wouldn't get out of the fire. You are great Cas, and I am glad you have Emma." He smiled at Cas. "Then there is Emma who is like my other little sister. I love you and am so glad you two finally figured out that you need each other because Cadwell Harbor wasn't going to survive if you didn't settle down." Paul raised his glass higher. "To Emma and Cas and their little one. May you always be happy and love one another."

Next Year, Halloween, Magnolia Street

Emma brought the bowl of candy out to the table that they had placed on their new doorstep of the rebuilt Brewster home. It was a replica of the one that had burnt down the year before.

She turned and kissed Cas, who had walked down to see how she was doing. Then he kissed the little bundle that was strapped to Emma. Their little Eliza had been born early but healthy. She was bald at the moment but there was a shadow of red hair coming. Her eyes were a beautiful brown.

"I just wanted to come and see how my two girls were."

Emma wrapped her arm around her husband. Then feeling something wrapping around her leg glanced down and saw it was one of the kittens born eight weeks earlier to Mika and Midnight. Some were black like the father or Torti like Mika.

Mika and Midnight sat watching the kitten, the one who Emma said she would keep.

She smiled at her familiars. Then turning back to Cas. "Have your crew come down after, for refreshments. We need to break in the new home with this Halloween."

Cas smiled. "Yes, a much nicer way than last year. I will see you after things wind down." He pulled Emma in tight as he could with the baby tucked in between the two of them. Kissing Emma's lips, he smiled against her lips when he heard her thoughts. *"I love you, Cas!"*

Cas smiled and kissed her one more time. "I love you too Emma. I am so thankful I have you."

Midnight watched as Cas walked up the street. Who would have thought Cas was a warlock. He was very happy to see his family growing, very happy indeed. He looked over at Mika. She had pinned their kitten down and was giving it a good bath. She looked up at him. Her gold eyes blinked at him.

"Don't even think of it. Do you realize if I have another litter I will be exhausted. These kittens are a handful and all of them act just like you."

Midnight looked up at Emma who laughed and patted his head. Yes, he was one happy familiar.

Books By Author Mary Moriarty

One Thousand Years to Forever
http://www.amazon.com/Thousand-Years-Forever-Beloved-Vampire-ebook/dp/B00EW4I89A/ref=sr_1_1?ie=UTF8&qid=1408631360&sr=8-1&keywords=One+Thousand+years+to+forever

https://www.smashwords.com/books/view/352794

I've Been Waiting for You
http://www.amazon.com/Been-Waiting-Beloved-Vampire-Book-ebook/dp/B00GTTTYHQ/ref=sr_1_2?ie=UTF8&qid=1408631590&sr=8-2&keywords=I%27ve+been+waiting+for+you

https://www.smashwords.com/books/view/380222

Redemption at Midnight
http://www.amazon.com/Redemption-Midnight-Beloved-Vampire-Book-ebook/dp/B00JTD9B72/ref=pd_sim_kstore_2?ie=UTF8&refRID=1FFBV8YAX6DB3QSK4YQ6

https://www.smashwords.com/books/view/431046

The Witchling Grows Up
http://www.amazon.com/Witchling-Grows-Family-Pendragon-Book-ebook/dp/B00M9QVL60/ref=pd_sim_kstore_1?ie=UTF8&refRID=0KHMEC7FXCS7BD3NZW76

https://www.smashwords.com/books/view/447931

Coming Soon

Her Protector- Book Three In the Family Pendragon Series, December 19th, 2014

Re-Issue of The Kings of Angkor: Army of a Thousand Elephants, February 19th, 2015

The Lioness, Romantic Suspense , April 16th, 2015

Love Beyond a Shadow of a Doubt, Book four of Family Pendragon Series , June 17th, 2015

Coming Soon, December 19th, 2014
"Her Protector" Book two in the Family Pendragon Series

The house was abuzz with activity. Windows were being thrown open to air out rooms long in disuse. Gardeners touching up the gardens.

The kitchen was a blur of activity as cooks and cleaners tried to make room for one another.

The Great Manor house of the Pendragon family was opened up and would soon see the family home after a long absence.

"What do you mean, you can't have that amount of meat here in that short a notice?" Emma listened to the voice on the other end and saw her sister Molly stirring up something. Her mother and grandmother were scurrying around with lists in their hands.

"I know this is short notice and it only gives you forty-eight hours, but I assure you if you don't help me in this time of need for this party we are throwing I will in the future bring our business elsewhere. No, Sir William is not here, or he would be calling." She listened and then took a sip of her tea. Made a face and waved her hand over the teacup. Took another sip and smiled. If nothing else her tea was going to taste decent.

She listened to the man on the other end. "No sir, I need all the organ parts also. No I don't think it matters what I need them for. I have quite a gathering of..." How could she say, every vampire available on the continent was coming, not to mention from the states and here in the UK. It would be the biggest gathering of creatures ever.

Emma scribbled a note and let it fly to her sister Molly. Molly looked at it and smiled.

"I'm on it as I speak." Molly whispered to Emma before walking out of the kitchen area. She walked out of the kitchen and up the back stairs to the main rooms. There she looked for the butler, Keats.

"Keats?" Molly spoke as she came into the main sitting room.

Branson Keats turned around to his name being called. "Yes Ma'am?"

Molly walked up to her cousin's butler, who had been in service for his whole life. Actually he had taken over for his father. Their family, though not creatures or from their coven, had been serving her family faithfully since before the Great War. The original Keats had been the family butler for her cousin William many years ago.

"Keats, we will be having deliveries these next few days. Please make sure the staff knows that it's the utmost importance that things get to their proper place immediately."

Keats bowed. "I understand we have many guests who are staying here before you all go onto Glastonbury."

"Yes, it seems our Dylan needs rescuing."

Keats knew as did his father and grandfather before him that he worked for a family of very powerful witches. It had been whispered that Lady Rose Pendragon was the granddaughter of one of the most powerful witches ever and descended from Morgan LeFay herself. He had always kept his thoughts to himself but with Molly here he would say his piece. "Ma'am, if I may be of any help ever, just let me know. I know I am not like you, But Lady Dylan was always my favorite and I wouldn't want anything to happen to her."

Molly was touched by Keats' remarks. She could remember when they would come as a family to visit her cousin William and how Dylan pretty much had the run of the house. "That's the reason why we are having this weekend house party, it's to bring in um, er, reinforcements to help in getting Dylan back."

Keats knew he wasn't necessarily a brave man but he did care what happened to Dylan. She was more like a sister or daughter he never had and would always cherish all the little gifts she was always bringing him when she was a small child.

"I would do anything to help that is, go with the ones." He knew and had heard of who was coming as guest this weekend, creatures of the night. Vampires who from all accounts, if he thought Sir William was a big man, these would dwarf him. "Go with the creatures, Ma'am. If you understand what I am saying

Ma'am."

Molly was touched by Keats' knowing sacrifice. "I will remember that Keats, but for now the only thing I need that I know you can accomplish is make sure the household staff has everything in readiness. Also assure all the maids they've nothing to fear from our guests that will be arriving."

Keats smiled a knowing smile. "How many are we expecting to stay here at Pendragon Manor?"

Molly mentally checked off all the vampires she knew personally, having met them at Annie and Travis's wedding. "Twenty will be staying in the manor house, then there are numerous others who will be staying in the cottages or nearby. Some will only be coming for the party. I will have the final guest list to you later this morning."

Keats nodded his head. 'That is fine Ma'am. Now if you will excuse me, I had better make sure the maids are airing out the bed chambers."

Molly nodded. "Let me know how your new housekeeper is getting on. Shouldn't she be doing that? If you feel she needs some help don't worry I can give her pointers."

Keats smiled. "She is upstairs now instructing some of the younger maids. I am sure she will be fine. She is my niece and has spent a great deal of time here when the house was open."

Molly smiled and looked down at her clipboard. "Fine, well I will leave you for now. Just ring if you need anything."

She was walking away when she heard Keats clearing his throat. "Yes Keats?"

"Remember Ma'am if you need anything, I offer myself to do whatever is needed to get her back."

Molly smiled. "I will remember, Keats. Oh and one more thing. We don't know if Sir William and Lady Rose will make the weekend gathering, we really do hope. Please make sure their rooms are all aired out and ready incase they do arrive."

Keats nodded. "Yes, Ma'am."

* * * *

Emma saw the number on her phone and knew it was Justice.

"Yes Justice, how far out are you from the manor?"

Justice glanced at his GPS and then at his watch. "I have about thirty minutes before arriving. I have her dragon with me and her two dogs."

"Speak for yourself Vampire." Max, Dylan's Chihuahua, was glaring at Justice from the door of his crate.

Justice grimaced. It had been quite a chore to get the little Chihuahua in the dog crate. He had been throwing threats ever since they had left London.

"I don't know why Nero and I had to leave Dylan's home in Glastonbury. We should be there in

case she gets away. She will want us home."

Justice listened to Emma and the little dog at the same time. "Hold on Emma, there is a disturbance in the car that needs to be dealt with."

He turned to the little crate that was on the front seat. On top of the crate slept the dragon. Justice saw the dragon open one eye and study him.

"Do you need help with little Napoleon?" **Tân asked with a sneer.**

Justice smiled at Dylan's dragon. "That would be so kind of you if you would help."

Tân smiled, stretched and then hung his head over the crate and proceeded to talk to the little dog.

Justice sighed. "I'm back. Now is there anything I need to know before arriving there?" He listened to Emma speaking low to someone in the back. Then heard her question.

Smiling, "I think all the vampires over one thousand years of age will be fine as far as needs go, as long as you have a herd of cattle, all will be fine. We will need that for the younger vampires with so many warm bloods in the house."

He smiled and looked at the road marker up ahead. "I will see you soon. Since HRH and his family will be arriving tomorrow I can help get the place in readiness for them. Ok, see you soon."

Justice drove and smiled. It had been harder to do anything but Cormac had assured him they would all help and go anywhere to get the Witchling, Justice's Witchling back.

Chapter 2

Justin, Brent and Bella drove along A38 to Plymouth.

Justin was at the wheel, Bella was sitting shotgun since she was pregnant as the riding made her quite carsick.

"Justin, would you be a dear and pull over for a second? I need a breath of fresh air."

Justin pulled over and Bella got out. Brent watched the love of his life bend over. Jumping out, he went and held Bella. He felt her start to heave so he put his hand on her forehead to give her something to brace herself on.

Bella finally felt she could stand. Standing up straight and turning into Brent's arms, she saw the concern written on Brent's face. "I will be fine. Father said one of our doctors would be there for the weekend and I can just rest."

Brent held his Bella close, marveling in his wife and soon to be mother of their child. She was so strong but he saw how she had suffered with this pregnancy. It was rare to see a vampire pregnant and that was another reason why the former king, Cormac, his father in-law, wanted this weekend to bring the two groups of creatures together. Maybe form an alliance and maybe future marriages. If Justice was to be mated to this witchling in the future, then maybe more of their kind would find a witch. Maybe the new blood would help with hereditary vampires being born.

Bella looked up into Brent's face. Standing on her tiptoes, she kissed his nose. "I will be fine, don't worry. I am sure the Goddess didn't allow me to become pregnant only to take me to be with her and leave you alone."

Brent kissed her forehead and took in her scents. "I will try not to worry. But it's hard."

Justin was getting antsy to get going. He didn't like garden parties and since this was something new for him, a weekend gathering with witches, he was even surer he wouldn't enjoy himself. With his mate back in Russia he had decided to go with his brother Brent and his Bella.

He envied them. They had a beautiful relationship. He and his mate's relationship was up and down, had been for the last few months. She had been the one to decide they needed time apart.

Justin watched his twin and Bella. They were close and communicated even by their looks to one another. There had never been that with Justin's Russian beauty. It had been a lot of sex and the constant round of parties. When he had said he would really like to find a quiet home in the country she had balked. He lay his head back and breathed deep. The only thing that took the yearning away was fighting or battle. Since he had not been overseas for months now, he couldn't even fight with his brother. He figured he would have to go on a hunt this weekend. Opening his eyes again, he looked out the window and saw Brent scooping Bella up and kissing her. He would like that someday. No, he would love that. Vampire or not, he had come from a loving family and he could only party for just so long. There came a time when one must settle down and start a family. Whether it be by adoption or by natural means. One last look at his brother Brent, Justin knew he wanted that.

Chapter 3

Odin and Sally drove down the small coastal road to Pendragon Manor.

Sally let her hand rest on Odin's, who kept his hand on the gearshift of his JAG.

"You know this will be the first time we will have been away from Fatima."

Odin smiled but kept his eyes on the road. He had never been this far southwest in England and this road was a bit tricky. He didn't want to miss the turn.

"She is fine. She will be running the castle before you know it. She has all the maids eating out of her hand not to mention the ghost."

Sally sighed. "I know, it's just so hard."

Odin took Sally's hand. "It gives us some time alone, so to speak. We have had so little time alone. I for one am glad we have this weekend. Plus it will give us a chance to thank Emma Southwick again for helping us get rid of Gormflaith."

Sally turned to her husband and mate. Smiling, she let her finger trace his chin and let her finger tip rest on his lip.

"Don't start something you can't finish, Sally my dear, this vampire is in need of some real quality time with his mate."

Odin saw a small road off to the side. He took a sharp turn and they ended up on a small road that led to the ocean.

Bringing the JAG to a stop, he turned and pulled Sally towards him after she unbuckled her seatbelt.

He had her up on his lap as he slid his seat back. Grabbing her ass, she grabbed his face. He knew there would be no waiting for later. He wanted her now and he was going to have her.

Sally took Odin's face in her small hands and kissed him deep. Hearing the gentle purr come from her mate and husband she felt herself go like molten lava in seconds. Minutes ago she was worried about their daughter Fatima and now all she could think of was how fast she could get out of her clothes and make love to her husband and mate. She didn't care if her clothes got ruined. It wouldn't be the first time. What she knew was she needed to feel him inside of her right away. "Now!" she whispered as he tore her sweater from her body. "Now! I need you in me now, Odin."

Printed in Great Britain
by Amazon.co.uk, Ltd.,
Marston Gate.